JACK

DITS

TALL TALES
FROM THE MESS

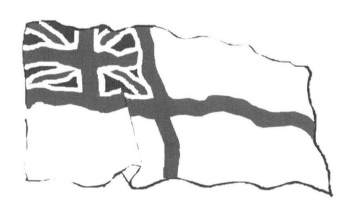

GEN DITS, GASH DITS
SHAGGY DOGS & DITTY'S

pwauthor@mail.com

INTRODUCTION

OFTEN, WRITING A PREFACE FOR A BOOK IS FAIRLY STRAIGHTFORWARD.

ONE SKETCHES A BRIEF OUTLINE OF THE CONTENTS, ADDS A FEW DETAILS WITHOUT GIVING TOO MUCH AWAY, FINISHING WITH A PERSONAL OBSERVATION OR TWO.

THAT'S ABOUT IT.

HOWEVER, FROM TIME TO TIME ALONG COMES A BOOK WHERE THIS IS NOT SO EASY, NOT SO SIMPLE.

JACK'S DITS, IS ONE SUCH BOOK.

THERE IS MUCH TO SAY ABOUT THIS BOOK AS IT STRADDLES, BY ITS VERY NATURE, MULTIPLE AREAS OF INTEREST AND RECOGNITION. THE WHYS AND WHEREFORES OF ITS CONCEPTION, THE ORIGINATION AND COLLATION OF THE CONTENTS, THE IMPORTANCE OF ITS PLACE IN ROYAL NAVAL SOCIAL HISTORY, THE *'AIDE MEMOIR'* INFLUENCE ON OLD HANDS AND ITS RELEVANCE, GOING FORWARD, TO THE 'MODERN' ROYAL NAVY.

PRIMARILY, JACK'S DITS IS FUN.

IT IS AN ECLECTIC COLLECTION OF HUMOROUS YARNS, FABLES AND ANECDOTES; MANY HAVE BEEN REGALED AGAIN AND AGAIN, FOR YEARS ON END, PASSED DOWN FROM GENERATION TO GENERATION OF SAILORS, FROM SHIP TO SHIP AND BACK AGAIN.

THE TELLING OF EACH DIT BEING SUBTLY ALTERED, SHORTENED, ELONGATED OR ENHANCED, BY EACH INDIVIDUAL YARN SPINNER, TO SUIT THE MOOD AND OCCASION OF ITS TELLING.

FOR THOSE UNCERTAIN ABOUT WHAT A 'DIT' IS, ALLOW ME TO ENLIGHTEN YOU.

FIRSTLY, DO NOT CONFUSE A DIT WITH A DITTY. THE LATTER BEING A SONG, THE FORMER A SAILOR'S TALE.

THERE ARE THREE MAIN TYPES OF DIT.

A DIT.

A GEN DIT.

A GASH DIT.

A DIT IS A STORY WHERE THE TELLER AND THE LISTENERS HAVE NO INCLINATION AS TO THE AUTHENTICITY OF THE TALE BEING SPUN. IT MAY BE, POSSIBLY, FACT. EQUALLY, IT MAY BE A TOTALLY FICTITIOUS STORY.

A GEN DIT, IS A TRUE TALE, A STORY BASED ON REALITY. AT LEAST THIS IS HOW THE STORY IS PRESENTED TO THE AUDIENCE. EVEN IF THE SAILOR GIVING THE ACCOUNT HAS HIS OWN DOUBTS, HE WILL DO ALL WITHIN HIS POWER TO MAKE THOSE LISTENING BELIEVE HIS PARABLE IS FACTUAL.

A GASH DIT IS PRECISELY THAT, GASH, RUBBISH, FABRICATION. THESE FALSEHOODS ARE OFTEN TOLD TONGUE IN CHEEK, OR WITH GREAT GUSTO, KNOWING THAT NO ONE, THE SPEAKER OR THOSE LISTENING, BELIEVES A SINGLE WORD. THEY ARE SPUN PURELY FOR ENTERTAINMENT, TO ELICIT A GRUNT OR A GROAN ON COMPLETION.

WHAT IS OFTEN THE CASE, WITH ALL OR ANY OF THESE FORMS OF DITS, IS THAT GEN DITS ARE OFTEN GASH DITS AND DITS; WHICH ARE DITS THAT CAN BE GASH DITS OR GEN DITS, OR MAY WELL JUST BE DITS AFTER ALL. GASH DITS ARE ALWAYS GASH DITS UNLESS THEY ARE FOUND TO BE GEN DITS, OR INDEED JUST DITS.

OF COURSE, SOME DITS, ARE ALSO SHAGGY DOGS, ALTHOUGH THESE ARE OFTEN GASH DITS, SOMETIMES THEY ARE ONLY DITS. UNLIKE BLACK CATS, WHICH ARE MOSTLY GEN DITS, BUT COULD BE EITHER GASH DITS OR DITS.

IN JACKS DITS, I HAVE INDICATED, WHEN PLAUSIBLE, IF A DIT HAS BEEN PRESENTED AS A GEN DIT OR A GASH DIT. ALL OTHER DITS IN JACKS DITS ARE TO BE ASSUMED AS DITS. ALTHOUGH, I CANNOT

CONFIRM THE VALIDITY OF ANY DIT BEING ANYTHING OTHER THAN A DIT. WHEREAS THE JOKES AND DITTY'S INTERSPERSED BETWEEN THE DITS OF ALL TYPES, ARE INDEED JOKES AND DITTY'S.

I AM GLAD THAT HAS NOW BEEN MADE CRYSTAL.

THE IDEA OF CREATING **JACK'S DITS** CAME ABOUT FROM THE MANY WONDERFUL COMMENTS AND MESSAGES I RECEIVED AFTER THE PUBLICATION OF *'THE PUSSERS COOK BOOK'*, IN WHICH I INCLUDED A FEW DITS AND ANNOTATIONS FROM SOME OF THE OLD HANDS.

IT WAS ASKED OF ME IF I COULD PUBLISH A BOOK WHICH WOULD KINDLE MORE RECOLLECTIONS, STORIES OLD SALTY SEA DOGS COULD REMINISCE OVER.

I DECIDED TO MIX DITS AND JOKES, ALONG WITH A DITTY OR TWO, AS IT WOULD GIVE SUCH A TOME A GOOD BALANCE OF ENTERTAINMENT WHILE PROVIDING THE RIGHT STIMULUS FOR EVOKING FOND MEMORIES.

IT IS THESE, *'TALL TALES FROM THE MESS'*, WHICH ARE FONDLY KNOWN AS **JACK'S DITS.**

THIS BOOK IS NOT ONE WHICH SIMPLY AND ONLY HARKS BACK IN NOSTALGIC FASHION TO THE PAST, **JACK'S DITS** IS AN AUTHENTIC VALIDATION, A HISTORICAL RECORD OF ROYAL NAVAL SOCIAL HISTORY; ONE TOLD BY THE VOICES OF THOSE WHO SERVED. IT IS A TRUE AND GENUINE RECORDING OF LIFE DURING THE ROYAL NAVY'S HEYDAYS, THE LATE 1950'S THROUGH TO THE EARLIER PART OF THE 1980'S.

I VERY MUCH DOUBT **JACK'S DITS** WILL EVER WIN ANY ACCOLADES FOR POLITICAL CORRECTNESS, WHICH IS DEFINED AS:

'THE AVOIDANCE OF FORMS OF EXPRESSION OR ACTION THAT ARE PERCEIVED TO EXCLUDE, MARGINALIZE, OR INSULT GROUPS OF PEOPLE WHO ARE SOCIALLY DISADVANTAGED OR DISCRIMINATED AGAINST'.

ON THE CONTRARY.

JACK, IN HIS WISDOM, SOUGHT AT EVERY OPPORTUNITY, TO HIGHLIGHT THE DIFFERENCES, ABNORMALITIES, ODDITIES AND STRANGE TRAITS OF EACH AND EVERY INDIVIDUAL.

THE ABILITY TO ACCEPT AND THEN LEARN TO REFRACT, DEFLECT AND RETURN INSULTS, OFFENSIVE STATEMENTS, SLURS AND SLIGHTS MADE JACK STRONGER, FOUNDED AND STRENGTHENED BONDS BETWEEN INDIVIDUALS, MESSMATES, OPPOS AND THE ANDREW ITSELF.

THOSE NEVER EXPERIENCING MILITARY ENVIRONMENTS I DOUBT SHALL EVER BE ABLE TO CONCEIVE THE STRENGTH OF THE BOND FORMED DURING SUCH COMRADESHIP. THE UNITY, LOYALTY AND SOLIDARITY CREATED BY SUCH A BROTHERHOOD.

JACK'S DITS REFLECT THAT BOND.

WITHIN THE WORDS OF THESE TALES LIE CLUES TO THAT IDENTITY, WHICH IS WHY THIS BOOK CONTAINS OBSCENITIES, IS SEXUALLY EXPLICIT AND OFTEN VULGAR. IT IS THE WAY THINGS WERE, IT WAS THE VERY ESSENCE WHICH MADE THE ROYAL NAVY, THE BEST NAVY IN THE WORLD.

A NAVY I WAS PROUD TO BE PART OF.

PAUL WHITE,

EX-R.N.

When Customs call

Gen

Watching a program on television, involving Custom

and Excise, had me reminiscing about returning to the UK after a 9-month deployment.

There was, as usual when returning home, an underlying atmosphere of excitement permeating throughout the whole ship.

Many of the married men wore an expression of worry on their faces, as they queued outside of the sickbay, praying their final small arms inspection was given the all-clear.

As Eddystone Lighthouse came into view over the horizon, so did the Customs Launch.

The sight of sniffer dogs standing on the launches bow sent a ripple of semi-panic through certain segments of the ship's crew and an unusual rush for the heads.

As usual, the Customs officers made themselves a temporary 'office' in the junior rating's dining hall. They sat behind a line of tables to inspect Jack's ill-gotten gains from the trip.

These were the usual random collection of cocky-watches, electronic gizmo's, gizzits and the prezzie's brought for the family in some far-flung shite-hole.

NOTE: Customs on Her Majesty's Ships work like this: -

The crew are required, usually in alphabetical order, to present themselves to the customs officers, declaring and/or showing items, which have been purchased, (or otherwise acquired) during the trip. These items are given a cursory assessment and a correspondingly token amount of revenue is collected from each sailor until Customs has collected the required amount they have been ordered to collect from the ship.

The government gets its revenue, Jack gets a receipt and can carry said items out of the dockyard without getting in the shit.

It is a painless exercise that leaves all parties involved happy and satisfied.

However, not every sailor is blessed with bountiful intelligence.

One lad, a keen photographer saved a small fortune and limited his runs ashore, until we docked in Hong-Kong, where he spent that small fortune on a shed load of photographic equipment.

He brought, many filters and other whatsits and thingamabobs, several state-of-the-art lenses; one so large and powerful you could see a fly's bollocks banging together as it flew... from a mile away.

All this was packed neatly into a special padded aluminium protective case, with the profile of each item cut into the interior protective foam, where they sat safely and snugly until required.

The young skin was proud of his gains, and rightly so.

Giving this equipment a cursory glance, the Customs Officer commented that it looked to be worth about £20.

The young lad's mouth fell open in shock. He began to protest, saying all the equipment was genuine and therefore worth more.

Cutting him short, the Customs Officer then said, oh...well, in that case, we will estimate its value at £25 pounds then. He winked at the baby sailor as he made this statement.

This led to an outraged outburst from the skin, who gave a huge figure, the price he actually paid for his collection when purchased in Honky Fid.

(Although this amount was a bargain, as it was considerably less than the price one would have paid in the U.K., the 'true' value was not the case in point.)

Shrugging, the customs officer then gave the skin a massive duty charge, based on the figure the boy blurted out. It was many times greater than he would have paid if his pride had not overruled his brain.

I guess, when he reads this dit, he will know how much of a tosser he was...

Just saying.

Frying Eggs

Joke

An Ex-matelot applies for a cook's job at the Hilton Hotel London.

Head chef asks him if he can fry an egg.

Matelot puts a rubbish bin either side of the cooker and a frying pan on the gas.

He throws an egg in the air, bounces it off each shoulder, bounces it off each kneecap, flicks it in the air with his foot, as it comes down he headbutts it, causing it to crack open, half the shell goes in one bin and a half in the other bin.

The egg falls into the frying pan doesn't break and he fries the perfect egg... The head chef cannot believe what he has just witnessed and musters all the staff into the kitchen to witness what he has just seen.

The man repeats the actions again and at the end, there is rapturous applause from the staff and the head chef.

Matelot says, "Thank you, do I get the job?"

"No" the head chef replies... "you fuck about too much".

A whole Ton of Lights

Gen

This dit refers, I believe, to HMS Fittleton. But I shall stand corrected, should you know better.

Due to a bad storm, the Old Man took us into Dundee,

Tying up at Victoria Dock we found there was little more doing that night because the weather was set for the next few hours, so went ashore to have a quiet 'session'.

We paid a visit to Bally's and the Unicorn and possibly one or two, or three other such salubrious establishments along the way.

On the way back to the ship, we spotted lots of flashing lights and, rather like moths are attracted to a flame, we *slightly inebriated sailors*, found the sight of these twinkling illuminations irresistible and crossed the road to investigate.

It turns out the Dundee city council were removing or repairing some old railway lines which, as it happens, ran the entire length of the dockside roadway.

The lights were placed there a safety precaution, warning people and drivers of the uneven surface, the potholes and other obstructions along the way.

We took all those lights. I think we counted over 40 of them if I recall correctly.

The following morning, as we sailed out into the North Sea, where we messed around for several hours.

On return, as we approached the Firth of Forth, the sun was about to set.

I recall the sky and clouds were an amazing show of colours; dappled amber right through to a hazy purple.

We watched until the sun finally dipped below the horizon, allowing the darkness of night to highlight our Ton-class minesweeper, which was slowly sailing under the bridge, with 40 orange flashing lights flickering on her decks.

We stashed them away before docking in Rosyth.

Eventually ditching them overboard when the batteries died.

From Russia with ~~Love~~ Sex

Dit

This is a tale from way back when everyone with a slightly eastern European accent was regarded as a spy.

Red's under the bed and all that codswallop.

There were Russian '*trawlers*' were everywhere in those days.

This dit is about how I became a spy!

It was 1969 and we had completed the Naval exercise "Deep Furrow", which took place in the Med with the Eagle, Ark and the cruiser, Blake.

At the end of the Deep Furrow, the lower deck was cleared in all ships present, to witness the first ever *'at sea'* deck landing of a Hawker Harrier 'jump jet'. I think this version was known as a Sea Harrier, but that may have been later?

However, the plane came and parked itself on the arse end of Blake to a huge applause and an air of disbelief in what had just been witnessed.

Then it was starburst for the fleet with ships popping off to all destinations for whatever jolly they were destined.

We were coming home to de-commission, so we got Gib as our stop-off en-route back to Blighty.

Strangely, so did that Russian trawler which had been doing second plane guard on the Ark!

Now, this is where things become interesting. On my first night ashore, I met a five-foot-eight blond woman who was as fit as shit.

Olga, no crap, that was her real name, was one very tall, beautiful... Russian woman.

I trapped her in a bar called "La Pulverin?" and around eleven o'clock that night we ended up on board a Russian *"Survey ship"*

Olga plied me with vodka, food and sex. All night, sweaty body wrestling type of, marathon length, sex.

Now, if she asked, whilst she was slobbering over my pecker, any pertinent questions I would most probably divulge every secret about British gunnery I knew... which would have taken about thirty seconds, as I was a ship's cook!

Olga and I did talk when we did not have some part of the other's body in our mouth. But like most people, we spoke about anything and everything, except ships and stuff.

Oh, and there was no pillow talk in our sleep because we didn't get any sleep, not a single zed.

At silly o'clock the next morning, I managed to escape Olga's clutches, with just enough time to leg it across the mall and get aboard without being adrift.

However, as I enter the dockyard I am waylaid by a bunch of reggies

Dragged off, I soon found myself in a dank little room in some nondescript building and they commenced grilling me.

They had a big lamp, like the ones you see in films during an interrogation. I almost pissed myself at the amateur dramatics of it all.

Now, I am unsure if you know, but those lights generate quite a bit of heat and such heat tends to regenerate latent sexual odours.

I had not been given the chance to dhoby, so the tiny room we are in soon starts to smell a bit like Billingsgate fish market.

It was either the smell of fanny or the cooks were boiling up some Spithead pheasants for breakfast.

Having decided it was nothing to do with the galley, the Reg says, "If you cooperate, we will let you dhobi that fucking stench off."

"Are you kidding?" I say, "it took all night to get it like this and my oppos will wanna sniff before I wash it off."

"The dirty fuckers," he says.

"You know them, then?" I said, pissing myself laughing.

It was late in the afternoon, after hours of interrogation by the Reggies and SIB before I am told to fuck off.

That night, in a small hotel in Gibraltar, the downfall of capitalist society was being plotted vigorously. Well, I am sure that was what those Reggies would have wanted, but what was really happening is Olga and I were at it like rutting dogs again.

I still remember my nights with Volga Olga as if it were yesterday.

It didn't seem much of a 'cold war' to me while I was in Gibraltar for those few days.

If Olga had been on the hinge of defecting, I think I would have said, "count me inski, comrade."

Tennis?

Joke

Yesterday while leaving the tennis courts, I noticed two tennis balls lying by the side of the fence.

I picked the balls up, put them in my pocket and proceeded on my way.

Walking towards my car, I noticed a beautiful blonde standing close by.

"What are those big bulges in your tennis shorts?" she asked with a smile.

"Tennis balls," I answered, smiling back.

"Wow," said the blonde, looking upset. "That must hurt. I once had tennis elbow and the pain was unbearable."

A Port Stanley Rover

Confession

Some might say it was me, (H.R.), who drove a two-ton Argentinian Land Rover around Port Stanley that evening.

The Argentine Land Rover which somehow ended up, nose to tail, with its sister Land Rover like they were kissing.

Just stopping short of the embarkation jetty.

Some might say it was me, which was why I spent a night in the cells at the Governor's house.

In the morning, I was found not guilty. (*Some may say on a technicality*).

But I was found not guilty and not guilty is an exoneration of all charges.

Happy daze, indeed.

Call Me

Joke

I was at the pub yesterday when one of the barmaids asked me what my ring tone was.

"Light brown like everyone else," I replied.

Women these days seem far more forward than they used to be.

Original Navy sayings... (*Part 1*)

At loggerheads

Loggerheads were hollow spheres of iron, one at each end of a shaft.
They were heated and used to melt tar in large tubs. The expression arose because two loggerheads can never come together.

True colours

Naval etiquette allowed false colours, (*flags*) to be displayed when approaching an enemy ship, Yet, insists true colours were flown once the battle is engaged.

Above board

The expression 'all above board', refers to things on the top deck of the ship and, therefore, freely open to inspection.

A Recipe for Disaster

Dit

ake one lanky tall streak of piss type Scouse cook.

T

Add a short arsed, egg on legs style Scouse PO cook.

Plus, one average leading cook. Mix in a large quantity of alcohol... and one rather large, hot, deep fat fryer....

The result? As the evening progressed the two Scouse's begin to argue, again, over fuck all.

The tall one tries to put the fat one's head into the deep fat fryer.

The leading cook is laughing, thinking it is simply a joke.

But by the time the two Scouse's are separated, the PO has a burnt hand.

Things quieten down after that and, eventually, everybody turns in.

The tall Scouse cook is given an early shake, for morning watch. (B*reakfast Cook*).

He asks the lower deck trot what time the short arse Scouse cook is to be woken, volunteering to do the wake-up call himself.

At the appropriate time, the Tall cook shakes the fat cook awake, with a rolling pin and loud, "**WAKE UP YOU LITTLE SHIT**".

Result: 1 broken arm, 2 dis-ratings and one 28days DQ's.

What the Doc said

Joke

Whenh I last saw the sickbay Doc, he said, "Don't eat anything fatty".

I asked the Doc if that meant I needed to cut eating chips from my diet?

He looked at me over the top of his horn-rimmed glasses and said, very slowly...

"No... don't - eat - anything - for - a - week, Fatty".

Some of Murphy's Laws

The things that come to those who wait, maybe the things left by those who got there first.

Give a man a fish and he will eat for a day. Teach a man to fish and he will sit in a boat all day drinking beer.

Flashlight: A case for holding dead batteries.

God gave you toes as a device for finding furniture in the dark.

When you go into court, you are putting yourself in the hands of twelve people, who weren't smart enough to get out of jury duty.

A little 'oggin

A Gen Deps Dit

W e were steaming on the top.

The weather took a turn for the worse and become as rough as a badger's arse.

So, it was into the tower and then back inside where it was warmer and a lot less wet.

It was a simple matter of closing the top hatch, opening the lower and clambering down.

But the Elephants footprint was not in place.

As I came through the lower, the OOW noticed some 'oggin coming in and ordered a matey to grab a bucket, stand below and catch the drips.

As the last man came through the upper hatch, a great gopher came over, forcing the top hatch down, but not before dumping a great deal of the wet stuff inside the tower.

The man managed to lift the lower hatch and a ton of 'oggin crashed down on fellow me laddie below with his pathetic one-gallon bucket.

Tossing the bucket unceremoniously across the deck, he shuffled off mumbling about something fucking something or other, knob jockey, twating, bastards.... his voice eventually fading away as he disappeared down the passageway.

Then it was all hand on before the water reached the battery.

Great days!

Doha, Qatar

Gen Dit

I was walking through Doha airport, towards my departure gate, when an attractive African lady smiles at me and asks if I want a whore.

OMG, I thought. I never expected to be accosted at the airport, surely, they should not allow that sort of thing here.

So, I say, "No thanks, I am a married man."

She seemed to look at me strangely, even a little confused.

I kept walking and soon passed a sign which said, "Lahore."

What a Muppet.

Jam

Here is a short one from long past, even way before my time.

It is not told so often nowadays I'm sure, but well worth an outing in Jack's Dits, if only for posterity.

An OD and a Bootie are bessie oppo's.... (*Yes, it's fictional!*).
The Booty is RA in Pompey, both stationed at Whale Island.
One day the Booty invites Jack up homers for tea.

Jack accepts the offer.

The Booty tells Jack, that his Mother is a stickler for good manners, so Jack must be on his best behaviour and he is to watch his language.

Jack, not wanting to miss out on a few free stickies, agrees.
A few hours later they are sat in florally patterned armchairs.
The Booty's mother pouring tea into china cups.

She has laid out a plateful of freshly sliced bread, little curls of butter, china pots with homemade lemon curd, marmalade and jams.

Another plate is piled high with freshly baked butterfly cakes and Battenberg laid on paper doilies and sitting in the centre of the coffee table.

Jack looks at the Booty and says, "Pass the fucking posy, will yer".

The Booty looks at Jack and reminds him, in no uncertain words, about his language.

"Oh, yeah," says Jack, "Sorry 'bout that"... "Pass the fucking Jam, will yer, please".

P.H. and the Masked Man in Black.

Gen (ish)

B ack in the eighties, while onboard HMS ??, a Killick

Seaman was the duty of Quartermaster on this particular evening. We were berthed in Gibraltar.

As part of his Quartermaster duties, the Killick was responsible for ensuring everyone who came aboard ship was authorised to do so. Following the correct procedure, he checked everybody's identity card as they reached the top of the gangway. In addition, he showed the expected diffidence and respect for officers as they returned to the ship.

Ratings who regularly undertake Quartermasters duties tend to recognise most of the ship's company. Even so, this Killick was a diligent soul and as he was often watched over by the duty officer, he took his role seriously and his Quartermastering was done by the book... although which book is a question best not asked.

Late one evening, just before the end of his watch this Killick spotted a dark figure trotting up the gangway. This person was clad in black motorcycle leathers and wearing a black motorcycle helmet with one of those darkened visors. He looked a like a Darth Vader type Astronaut. *(Although Darth Vader had not been created at this point in time, you'll get my drift.)*

Although modern terrorism did not exist and the threat from the IRA was not really one which was targeted at the Royal Navy, it was still correct to carry out proper security checks. A threat, however unlikely it might be, was still a possibility. Something our dutiful Killick was conscientious enough to realise. Besides, as Quartermaster, he loved flexing his 'pissed with power' muscles.

As the leather-clad figure approached the quartermaster's station he did not even glance in the Quartermasters direction but continued to walk towards the hatch to enter the ship. Our dutiful Killick stepped in front of the person and, holding his arm out, blocked the figures passage.

"Can I see your ID card please mate?" asked the Killick, holding out his hand expectantly.

The figure attempted to sidestep him, ignoring the Quartermasters request for his identity card.

Once again, the Killick stood in front of this mysterious, black-clad figure with both arms outstretched blocking all progress. "Can I see your ID card please?" He spoke loud and clear, enunciating each word.

It was at this time the Quartermasters relief arrived, ready to take over his duty so our stalwart Killick could grab some scran. He stood beside the Quartermaster, making any attempt to skirt around him by the black-clad Darth Vader futile. *(Or am I mixing my Sci-fi characters a bit!)*

Anywayhow, the leather-clad figure leant towards our Killick, black visored helmet level with his eyes.

"What is your problem, QM?" he grunted, "I don't have time for all this shite."

"I need to see your ID card, please mate," was the simple. reply, as he fought to keep his cool and professionalism.

The leather-clad figure huffed and puffed and, after an immense amount of fishing around for his wallet in a myriad of zipped-up pockets, produced a Royal Navy identity card declaring him to be a Lieutenant somebody or other.

Noting the Rank shown on the I.D card, our gallant Killick stood smartly to attention and saluted.

But, as he did he asked. "Would you kindly remove your helmet, sir?"

"What?"

"Your helmet, sir. You must remove it, so I can confirm this person shown on this I.D. card is actually you, the bearer of the said card." The Killick stated, still holding the lieutenants I.D. card in his sticky mitt.

Our Killick was clearly enjoying this moment. Particularly as now there was a large group of lookers-on and loafers who had amassed onto the deck and were enjoying the confrontation.

The Lieutenant was clearly unused to such insistence from a subordinate. Still standing in front of our Killick, the Lieutenant puffed up his chest and raised his head.

The crowd, which was now like a packed audience in a theatre, seemed to hold their breath in unison, waiting with anticipation for the scene to unfold.

Like the unveiling of the aforementioned Darth Vader, the Lieutenant slowly removed his helmet.

"Are you happy now?" questioned the Lieutenant from a face boiling red with rage, his eyes firmly fixed on the Quartermaster.

Keeping his cool, the Q.M. simply said. "Yes, Sir. Thank you, Sir. I am satisfied the ID card belongs to you."

The Quartermaster smiled at the officer and held out the ID card to returned it.

The lieutenant snatched it from the Killicks grasp and, poking him in the chest with a bony fingertip asked, "What's your name?"

"Leading seaman **** ******, sir."

"Well, Leading Seaman **** ******," said the Lieutenant, "you bloody well stand to attention when you address me, do you hear me?"

"Yes sir," said the Killick, straightening himself and standing as tall as he could.

"How long have you been on this ship?" The Lieutenant questioned.

"About eighteen months now, sir." Answered the Quartermaster.

"And I have been on this ship for a year and nine months, yet you don't know who I am?" The Lieutenant asked raising his arms in the air, gesticulating to the onlookers. It was clear the Lieutenant was enjoying his moment in the limelight too.

"No, sir," said the Killick honestly, "I do not recognise you, sir."

"I find that difficult to believe. Do you not know what happens onboard this ship? You are pathetic. I will be speaking with your Divisional Officer. When does your watch end?"

"Now Sir," said the Killick.

"Right, report to me at my cabin in thirty-five minutes." The Lieutenant stormed off, ducking through the hatchway and disappeared into the dark interior of the ship.

The Killick sighed and said, "What the fuck was all that about?" to his oppo's

"Fuck knows, mate." Was the general consensus.

Within seconds the Lieutenant was back, stepping back through the hatch he entered moments ago and marching across the deck.

The Q.M. heard someone say, "Oh, fuck shit, his back."

The dispersing crowd reformed at a safe distance. Another voice said "Ding, Ding. Round two, seconds away."

Our gallant Killick turned towards the officer, ready to face the wrath of this lieutenant once again.

To his surprise the officer walked past, his head held low trying not to make eye contact with anyone on deck as he made his way to the gangway.

"Can I help you, Sir?" The Quartermaster questioned again, this time speaking loudly so he could not be ignored.

"Sorry, QM. Wrong ship," said the lieutenant, almost running down the gangway with echoes of raucous laughter reverberating from the bulkheads and seemingly following the officer through the dockyard to his own ship.

Soup, Sarnies and wet Knicks

Some of you oldies may remember this tale, from the old 'T class' boats in the 60's.

A baby chef was turned to in the galley, making soup and sarnies for nine o'clockers, when the skipper decided to snort.

The lads closed up and the boat was duly brought up to P.D.

The skipper mounted the scope and was having an all-around look at what was on the roof.

The baby chef was working in white light in the galley, on leaving to go to the for'd mess with the fanny of hot soup, put the light off, opened the curtain, which hung over the top half of the galley door and set off carefully feeling his way for'd.

He was blind as a fuckin bat of course, after coming from the brightness of white lighting.

The skipper was swinging around on the periscope and chef got a hefty thump as the old man turned around, the soup went tits up, all over the skipper's feet, which prompted the said captain to yell the infamous "Fuck you, mind my feet."

The Plainsman, in the ensuing chaos, shouted to the forends to flood Q and then put twenty degrees of dive on, to get to 90 ft. in response to the old man's rather sharp command.

The resulting fiasco could have had dire consequences, as the said boat ended up at 250ft with the snort mast full of wet stuff overflowing into the control room.

A few wet knicks later, the exercise was resumed successfully and everyone lived to tell the tale.

P.S. *Deep diving test pressure on the old T class had been reduced to 200ft depth,* **(50ft less than we found ourselves at that day)** *by the 60's.*

A sneaky Run Ashore

Gen

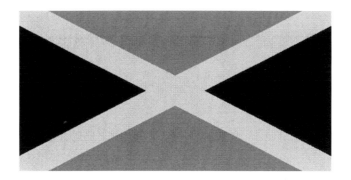

This one is from way back, from about 1963 I think.

I was under stoppage of leave when visiting Jamaica.

After the last muster, I was up and over the stern to jetty quicker than the proverbial rat-up-a-drainpipe.

A quick run up the far (*dark*) side of the warehouse, where my oppo was waiting for me in Taxi, engine running, ready for a quick getaway.

Great night on the pop.

Luckily, I managed to get back onboard and down to the Mess, pretty much a reverse of the way I went ashore in the first place, before call the hands.

Thanks to another oppo of mine, Janner.

He was a good mate and distracted the gangway staff, which was by the Torpedo tubes, during my escape and sneaky return.

Oh, those glory days of mine!

Naked

Joke

Wife gets naked and asks hubby,

"What turns you on more, my pretty face or my sexy body?"

Hubby looks her up and down and replies,

"Your sense of humour!"

The Train Driver

A Gen Veterans Dit

My last boat was the Churchill. After leaving the Mob I worked on the railways.

As it happens... I was awarded the Queens Jubilee Medal because I was one of the regular Royal Trains drivers.

It was the Queens Equerry who presented my medal. I was wearing my Submariners tie for the occasion.

The Queens Equerry nodded at my tie and said, "Submariner".

I did not know what to say, I think the sense of occasion had got to me. So, I simply called him a "Skimmer".

Returning to my seat, my wife said, as I sat down, "I can't believe you called him a Skimmer."

This is a genuine true dit, lucky I never called him an Airy Fairy.

Singing...

If you have a daughter.

Bounce her on your knee.

If you have a son.

Send the bastard off to sea

Singing bell-bottom trousers,

coats of Navy blue.

Let him climb the rigging,

like his Daddy used to do!

Some deflated ardour

...or a tale about a stoker's tail

For reasons of anonymity during this dit, we shall call the stoker, Brian. (Gash Dit?)

B rian was a stoker, one who was not blessed with the

greatest amount of common dog. He was, however, linked by most of the ship's company.

One downside to knowing Brian; he was always skint and always looking for ways to make a few quid.

Brian was skint when we visited Keel, where, as it happened, they were holding a week-long beer festival.

Now, Germany was far more relaxed in those days regarding sexual activities and the sale of sex toys, than the laws back at home.

With that knowledge, along with knowing the personal frustrations experienced by an all-male crew during a long stint at sea, Brian decided he could make a killing by renting an inflatable doll to the ship's crew.

Yep... you are thinking what I am thinking. Let's be honest, even matelots will draw the line at some point. But Brian would not listen.

He made a sign, using brightly coloured felt tips It read along the lines of, *"Fifty pence a go & the first person to notice her nose running has to empty her."*

Not, I must say, a notice designed to stimulate sexual desire in most men.

While Brian was fairly unselfish, he felt it justifiable to spend the first night with the inflatable woman before he sold her into prostitution.

As most of us were temporarily billeted onshore, in as was often the case back then. It was to a small shite-hole hotel, we returned after a decent run ashore and some rather large quantities of German larger.

Pissed as farts, we decided to get our heads down for the few hours which were left before sunrise.

However,

We were disturbed by a strange, yet loud squealing noise echoing through the hotel.

Hearing doors banging and disgruntled voices, I went into the corridor to see what the noise and fuss was about.

I could see nothing, but the noise continued. So, I walked towards where the sound was coming from, as did my shipmates and a few of the other hotel guests.

On reaching a stairwell, we heard a German voice shouting. I do not speak the language, but could still tell from the tone, the man was not a happy bunny.

Walking down the stairs half a flight, I could see who was shouting. It was the hotel owner.

He was shouting at Brian.

Brian was naked, his spotty fat white arse pumping up and down. Beneath him, with arms as wide open as her mouth, was the inflatable latex doll.

As Brian thrust himself into the doll, her backside slid across the vinyl creating the loud screeching sound which had woken the entire hotel.

The hotel owner, (I found out later was called Otto), was holding back a rather large Alsatian dog. With one flick of his wrist, Otto let loose the dog.

The dog decided in its own doggy wisdom to attack the thing which was making the noise.

The dog's teeth sank into the doll hip, which let out a long farting noise as it withered into a wrinkled mess beneath Brian's sallow body.

"You twating bastard," Brian shouted as he stood, genitals swinging and pointing, in a half-deflated manner towards myself and Otto.

"You've burst my woman," he continued, before lunging towards Otto.

Luckily, two other stokers made an appearance and grabbed him. They dragged the kicking and screaming Brian, still dragging his deflated latex lover along the floor behind him, back to his room.

A few Schnapps and a whip-around got Otto to promise not to report Brian.

On the way back to my room, I looked into Brian's, to ensure he was well.

Brian was sitting on the edge of his bed with a bicycle puncture repair outfit trying to save the life of his girlfriend.

Another of Brian's fortune-making idea brought to an untimely end.

This, however, was not the last of Brian's adventures...

The day we sailed, I heard a huge roar from the stoker's mess, which was around the corner, past the after-escape tower.

Curious, I knocked and went into the stoker mess. Brian was standing on the mess table. He was naked from the waist down.

"What the fuck is it with you and getting your tackle out?" I asked.

When Brian turned around I could not stop myself from crossing my legs and wincing.

His foreskin was pierced by a large gold ring, I believe is called an Albert ring.

"You are off your fucking trolley," I said, shaking my head as I left.

Of course, the entire crew soon became aware of Brian's appendage. Everybody wanted to see it, but nobody wanted to ask.

On the birth of Prince William

Gen

Like all great British occasions connected with the Royal family, they are marked by the services in special, often traditional ways.

As it was, regarding observing the birth of HRH Prince William.

On that eventful day, I was duty PO at HMS Warrior, Northwood. The OOD was a young third officer Wren, with no idea regarding the routine a tot time;

Something I explained carefully and in detail to her.

We had, at our disposal, a couple of cases of Pusser's Rum. Some of which I opened and dutifully poured into the rum fanny, sampling each bottle, as required in QRRN's.

One of the details I shared with the OOD.

Sadly, the take-up of the tot was relatively poor.

As tot time neared its end I felt it was incumbent on me to chuck a few more bottles of Pussers finest into the fanny.

Just in case there was a last-minute rush.

I am afraid, at the end of tot time, there were several bottles worth or rum still in the fanny.

Our young OOD seemed somewhat bemused as what to do, turning to me for guidance.

I explained all the unopened bottles must be returned to the stores. The duty SA was duly summoned and the stock returned.

The Wren officer then enquired of the remaining rum still residing in the tot fanny.

I assured her I would follow past tradition and see it was disposed of in a seamanlike manner.

Happy her duties were over, she trotted off, presumably to the bun house for a G&T?

I hefted the tot fanny all the way to the Petty Officers mess, so I could keep my word and see that the remaining rum rations were, indeed, seen off in a most seamanlike, traditional fashion.

"God bless the Queen."

NBCD Briefing

Gen Dit

During an NBCD briefing on the upper deck, one instructor was addressing a group of run ashore hardened, members of the ship's company.

He asked them what they would do if they saw someone running around the upper deck, acting in a crazed manner, not wearing his respirator, foaming at the mouth, shouting incoherently with eyes glazed?

Came the reply, "I'd probably salute him, sir!"

Five of Murphy's Laws

1. Light travels faster than sound.

This is why some people appear bright until you hear them speak.

2. A fine is a tax for doing wrong. A tax is a fine for doing well.

3. He who laughs last thinks slowest.

4. A day without sunshine is like, well, night.

5. Change is inevitable, except from a vending machine.

Star-Shells and Khai

Gen

I was captain of the gun-house, which was x turret on the Leopard (*after turret*).

We were closed-up at action stations, up the ice, doing our Cod war bit.

The order came from the TS, that we, the turrets crews, could stand down for a while and take a breather in the gun-bay area.

I asked the Po GI in the TS if I could collect some Khai for the boys.

He said yes but, "make it snappy."

I bimbled off to the ops room because I knew them little ferkers always had a flask of Khai on the go.

Soon as I finished topping up my flask, the ferkin skipper shouted down from the bridge, "ok guns, light her up for me please."

Guns, who was a brilliant gunnery officer, looked at me, smiled, winked and said to the TS "ok ts x turret, two salvos starshell, at my mark."

I am legging it out the ops room with the Khai, I passed the skippers cabin down the main drag towards the gun-bay.

I am screaming "CLOSE UP FOR FERKS SAKE, STAND CLEAR HOIST AND RAMMERS, START THE GEN SERV PUMP, TURRET TO AUTO, GET THEM FERKIN STAR SHELL UP IN THE GUN HOUSE, NOW."

As the order came to shoot, I just managed to flick the gun switches to fire. This enabled the current to flow to the cordite, hence a big bang.

Starshell away, job done.

Later, when we stood down from action stations and talking to Guns, he just laughed and said, "I knew you would make it."

When I was a Skimmer

Gen

About 1975, when I was a Skimmer, on HMS Antrim.

We had a jolly into Liverpool.

Alongside us was HMS/M Valiant, or it may have been Warspite? My memory is not what it was.

Anyway...

Whichever one was alongside us, they had a major fire and we used all our firefighting gear to help put the blaze out.

(*Imagine the headlines now if a Nuclear boat caught fire in a British Port*).

The following day, we were due back to sea, but it turns out we can't leave Liverpool until we have replenished all our firefighting stock.

Hence another week alongside in the 'Pool'.

Shame... not.

Top run ashore.

A sing-along

Ditty

In a land where rum was tantamount to the daily good of the ship,
And OD's kept their fuckin place and badge men took no lip,
Where PC meant a constable, not some "correct" and fluffy rule,
And shaggin arse was optional, but not done as a rule.
Where women stayed behind on shore and the sea was man's domain,
To rove and drink and to sail and whore, till we came back home again.

Alas, it's now 'equality' and you've women along with the men,
It will never be the same at sea or even ashore again.
There gettin fuckin everywhere you can't get away from the fuckers,
How can you upend the board on their heads, when you're gettin dicked at Suckers?
It don't seem fair we blokes can't compete, they have taken over our life,
And who in the fuckin hell would want, a three-badge cunt for a wife?

Ah, bollocks I now have a plan and I think it would be great,
To let the bastards have it all and just wipe clean the slate.
They could do the work and fix the car and make sure we had money,
We'd stop at home whilst they went foreign and fuck would that be funny.
They could shag and drink and get the clap as we did back in yore,
In fact, if they made an allotment, they needn't come back any more.

Just send ickies, loads of them like we did in the day,
I wouldn't want that fuckin much, let's just say "half their pay".
I stop on Rowner, or St Beaudoux and live a life of ease,
Whilst they did what I used to do and roam the friggin seas,
And just like them in days gone by, when they stayed on the shore,
I'd fuck, and I'd shag and be a right fuckin slag, yes sir, a married patch whore.

Original Navy sayings... (*Part 2*)

Freeze the balls off a brass monkey

A monkey was the name given to a brass tray where cannon balls were stored.

In cold weather, the brass contracted, and balls fell off their stacks.

Let the cat out of the bag

The cat refers to the 'cat'o nine tails', a multi-tailed whip, used as a severe form of discipline.

The 'cat' as it was generally called, was kept in a cloth bag. Every sailor knew when it was taken out, there would be trouble.

Get out at Fratton

During intimate moments, Jack would be advised to wear a 'franger' (a condom), which were also known as a wellie, Fred, or forget-me-not.

If Jack did not have a 'franger', then his partner may expect him to *get out at Fratton*, the last railway station before Portsmouth and Southsea, which was the end of the line and the Royal Naval Dockyard in Portsmouth.

Flight deck Football

Too intense to be true? You tell me. Until then I'm categorising this as a Gash Dit.

But I still love it.

I would like to tell of an 'incident' during my time on

HMS Illustrious, on our voyage to the Falkland's in 1982.

I was 19 years old and extremely headstrong

My time on Lusty started by getting the ship ready for deployment. They were hectic, eighteen-hour days.

We sailed to Pompey for munitions where I was assigned to the magazines looking after torpedoes, sidewinders and a ton of other ships ammunition.

Life on the ship in those early days was hard, we carried everything on board by hand and ammo weighs a ton. We spent 36 hours in total getting it all on board.

We had no sleep and no rest for two days, my arms were dropping off and my legs were made of lead, but it had to be done so, we did it.

Baz, the workshop chief and a very likeable "*old school*" chief, said we should get some scran (*it was 08:30 and we had been up all night*).

I just stood there, closed my eyes and went to sleep.

The next few weeks were all GO, GO, GO. Sea trial after sea trial. Eventually, the ship was passed fit to fight, so we headed out of the docks and set sail for the Falklands.

At this point, the ship was heading for the Ascension islands.

We were about 100 miles off the coast of Africa when the captain announced we could have a "rec" day.

It was our first day off in over two months and it would be our last day off for another 3 months.

All the Harriers were in the hangar, along with the Sea King helicopters. This gave us the whole of the flight deck to enjoy as we wished. Clothing restrictions were relaxed, I wore trainers and shorts. it was hot enough to go without a T-shirt and the cooling breeze was welcome.

There was a 12 to 15-foot swell, but it made no noticeable difference to the mighty Illustrious as it cruised relentlessly southwards.

After sunbathing for an hour or so, I was getting bored and so were a couple of my mates, Dave and Geoff.

I decided to go down to our mess, where I found Al, with his head buried in a book. I asked if I could borrow his football, so we could have a kick about.

He said yes at first, but quickly retracted the offer when he found the hangar was full so it meant playing on the flight deck.

I pleaded with him to change his mind. "No, it cost me two quid."

I pleaded some more "I will give you two quid if we lose it."

He responded, "No, I can't replace the ball when we're at sea."

I was desperate, so I said, "If it goes over I will fetch it."

Reluctantly he agreed. I grabbed the ball before he changed his mind and legged it back to the flight deck.

Geoff and Dave were amazed I got Al's ball. I explained it wasn't easy and I promised to fetch it if it went overboard.

We formed a circle, some 20 yards from the edge and proceeded to pass the ball between ourselves. We passed, flicked and did keepie uppies between ourselves for 20 minutes or so.

Al came up to the flight deck to keep an eye on procedure and to guard his ball, while still reading his book.

Once the ball shot over my head, landing near to the edge of the deck. A PTI commented, "You'll lose that soon."

I disagreed and said, "NO chance."

Then Dave gave the ball a bit too much welly and it flew over the safety netting and into the Atlantic Ocean.

The PTI laughed and said, "Told you."

In an instant, I said, "we haven't lost it," and dived head first over the side.

It was a long way down. A trip which seemed to take forever.

Hitting the 'oggin was like taking a heavy slap on the top of my head. One of my arms took a bruising too.

It is surprising how far down you sink when jumping from that height. The journey back up took far longer and my lungs were bursting as I kicked and clawed my way up to the surface.

The tail end of the ship was just going by as my head broke free and I gasped for air.

I thought don't panic. The ball should be around here somewhere.

The sea had 12 to 15 feet swell, so when I was at the top I could see the ball. I reached it fairly quickly, relieved I had a buoyancy aid.

Geoff and Dave told me the PTI's faces went white as they watched me dive off the deck. *"You should have seen their faces."*

They ran down the flight deck shouting "***man overboard, man overboard, man overboard***".

The duty officer hit an emergency button releasing lifebelts from either side of the ships aft end.

With the aid of Al's football, I was floating without much effort, one minute I was atop of a wave and able to see the ship, the next I was surrounded by walls of water.

One of the lifebelts let out orange smoke.

Thoughts going through my mind were:

Do they know I am here? Of course, they do, the PTI's saw me. Why is the ship not turning about? Maybe they will send one of the sea kings?

Oh shit, I am in big trouble. Oh shit, I AM in big trouble.

I positioned myself in the lifebelt, using it more as a comfy seat than a lifebelt.

Although the ship was a long way off, I could still see hundreds of people all looking towards me.

I held the ball up, mainly to show Geoff and Dave I had got it, but also to re-assure Al it was safe (*all two-quid's worth of it*).

I was in the water for maybe half an hour when HMS Illustrious made its way back.

The crew were not happy. The small craft was struggling to cope with the swell. The cox'n told me to give him my hand but I was insistent he took the ball first.

"I have come this far, I am not going back without it," I bellowed when he told me to throw the ball away.

Back onboard, I threw the ball to Geoff. Al was nowhere to be seen.

I was ordered to report to the master at arms (*I was up shit creek without a paddle*).

A medic said I needed to see the medical officer first.

The sick bay was full, but not with patients. It was the entire medical staff who turned up for a nosy.

I stood outside the master at arms office, realising what I had done. I was thinking about what my mum and dad were going to say, they were so proud of me and now I had ruined it all in a split second.

Geoff said I should keep in touch once I was dismissed from service.

At that moment, the captain's steward appeared and told me I to see the captain.

"I can't, I've got to report to the master at arms."

"It's the captain," he replied smugly.

"OK, but what do I wear?" I was still in my shorts and trainers, both wet with salt water.

"Number two's, ASAP."

The mess held 15 blokes. It was crowded, even when half were on duty, so you can imagine what it was like with 30 or 40 blokes all asking me the same question.

Scrumps, one of three Killicks in the mess shook my hand and said, "it was nice knowing you, sad to see you go."

I grabbed a towel and headed for a shower.

The rest of the mess all rallied around as if I was a wounded soldier. One polished my shoes, another ironed a shirt for me, another guy lent me his cap, it was brand new and he had never worn it.

I knew nothing of this until I returned from my shower. Once dressed, more goodbyes followed and everyone wished me good luck.

I had never been on the bridge but was highly impressed. The captain swung around on his chair, removing his feet from the "dashboard" (for want of a better word) and held his hand out for me to shake.

My mind was racing? What is happening? Why aren't I being read the riot act?

"Br**den, isn't it?"

I shook his hand and stuttered my reply "y-y-yes, yes sir."

He carried on, "I think you should thank the first officer here, he steered the ship away from you once you fell overboard. "Well done for holding the ball in the air, it helped pinpoint your position. By the way, how did you fall over the side?"

Fell, fell, fell the word resounded around my head.

"Well... sir, it was like this, I was playing football on the flight deck when the ball flew over my head, I jumped to catch it and before I knew it, I am heading down towards the sea sir."

The captain then asked me if I was ok? I thought... ok? ok? I felt like I had won the pools (lottery)."

"Yes sir, a little shocked but ok sir, thank you, sir." I left the bridge with my adrenalin running again.

Wow.

I got away with it.

Wow.

First thing next day, I was summoned to see the Master at Arms. He called me into his office and informed me I was to be brought before the commander.

"But I saw the Captain yesterday and he thanked me for carrying out the correct procedure."

"WHAT," bellowed the Master at Arms.

I repeated my conversation with the Captain, to which his replied, "Get out, get out now, we'll see about this."

He was irate and he had every reason to be, but I had managed to avoid any punishment and although I knew I was a 'marked man', I had managed the great escape.

There was a buzz going around the ship and I could hear people saying, "that's him, the one who fell overboard".

The next few months were busy, but then it was all over and we were heading home.

Princess Margaret was asked to commission the ship and the Captain introduced me to her. I also got to meet Princess Anne.

Strange really, because I never spoke to Prince Andrew who served on Illustrious and also at Yeovilton whilst I was there.

Another few months passed and the captain was doing his rounds, but this time he wanted to ask me a question. "Did you get your cans of beer?"

"Beer sir? I haven't sir." He took out his handkerchief and tied a knot in it.

"I asked the publicity officer to get you some beer because he put the wrong name in Navy News."

I repeated myself, "No sir."

Half an hour later I was summoned to the master at arms office *(I had not done anything wrong so why is he after me)*.

"Here, he bellowed," and forcibly shoved 4 cans of beer into my ribcage. "Now get the fuck out of my sight."

Weather report

He said it was Gen

Bombing along on the surface, me, PO of the watch, plotting and dotting.

Officer of the watch bawls down to the helm.

Helm - bridge

Helm - sir

Bridge - weather report for the log

Helm - weather report for the log sir

Wind from the west, wind from the west sir.

Sea slight swell, sea slight swell sir.

Overcast, overcast sir.

Slight precipitation, slight percussion...

No helm, slight precipitation, slight prescription, (*OOW*

getting a bit arsey now)

No, helm, pay attention, slight per-sip-pit-tation.

Slight perspiration sir.

Helm - bridge

Helm - sir

Helm - bollocks to it, just put it down as raining a bit.

Roger sir, bollocks it's raining...........................

War Hero

Joke

As an elderly Stoker lay dying in his bed, suffering the agonies of impending death, he catches a whiff of Pussers rum wafting up the stairs.

Gathered what remaining strength he has, manages rolls off the bed. Leaning against the walls for support, he slowly made his way from the bedroom, and with every ounce of resilience he could muster, made his way down the stairs, gripping the bannister rail to aid his decent.

With laboured breath, he propped his feeble body against the doorframe, from where he could see into the kitchen.
Were it not for death's agony, the pain throbbing through his entire body, he would have thought himself already in heaven, for there, sitting on the table was a brand new, unopened bottle of Pusser's Rum.

Was this the final act of love and devotion from his wife of sixty years he wondered? Was this to see he left this world a happy man?

Mustering one great, one last final effort, he threw himself towards the table, landing on his knees in a crumpled heap. His parched lips parted, he could almost taste the tot before it was in his mouth.

The thought and the memory of the taste revived his determination, seemingly bringing him back to life. He reached out his aged and withered hand. It trembled on its way to the glass at the edge of the table.

A stick spatula, wielded by his beloved wife came smacking down, driving his hand away.

"Fuck off, " she said, "that's for the wake, after your funeral."

Pick it up and fuck off.

This is one memory of Andrew life that still puts a huge grin on my face, although it must be said, not if I am anywhere near a submarine.

I was spare crew at Dolphin.

They did not know what to do with me and soon ran out of naff ideas to *'keep me busy'*, so they sent me on a leadership development course.

It meant going back to Greenies headquarters, HMS Collingwood.

I was the only submariner in a class of about thirty baby tiffs and one three badge killick medic who simply waiting around so he could claim his pension.

The amount of stick I got, as a lone sun dodger, you can only guess at.

Anyways...

I was RA, living in the new forest about thirty-five miles away from the base. Each day I tried to be first in the queue to get out.

For those who don't know, Collingwood in those days was famed for training the rest of the worlds Navy's in electrical knowledge and had about 4000 places. If you were not near the front of the queue, it cost you a good half an hour before you even got out the gate.

Back then, the Reg staff searched nearly everybody to see if they were taking too many blueliners ashore and such like. This day, I was sitting in my car in the queue, waiting to get out of the main gate.

I was hoping the Joss-man would give me the nod and let me go straight through the gates.

Just then a killick chef named Bluey, came peddling past the long line of waiting cars on his push bike, he was RA at Rowner, and the sign says, as at all naval establishments, riders must dismount.

Well, Bluey lifted his right leg over his saddle as he dismounted, but caught the bikes saddlebag, which toppled the bicycle, the contents of the bags falling all over the deck. There was butter, meat and all sorts of stolen goodies from the galley.

Before the said contraband hit the road, Bluey shouted, "Who the fuck threw that shit at me?" looking back in the direction he came from.

The expression on the Jossman's face was priceless, he didn't move, he just said, "Pick it up Bluey and fuck off quick."

Caught in the trap

W hen *'Buster Brown'* was on the Ark, the cleaning party's mess was in 6 Tango 2.

The H/Q and store room just past 4 Alpha heads.

These heads were a semi-circle of traps, enabling 24 hairy-arsed matelots to have a good dump, in unison, whenever required.

One evening it was Buster's turn for round's.

"A4 heads ready for inspection, sir," he announced, as the DO arrived.

The duty officer said something along the lines of the usual crap, "where's your career going son."

Buster would give the expected answer, "down the bog sir."

Fortunately, for Buster, the duty pig on this day had a good sense of humour.

The traps were immaculate. Gleaming and pristine.

Not surprisingly, as they were the most important part of that great ship!

The traps doors were 'batwing' style, like the saloon doors in many 'wild west' movies; when the traps were occupied the lower part of the legs of the person using were visible.

On this day, the doors on one of the traps were closed. During rounds all the traps should have the doors open, so the inspecting officer had a clear and unobstructed view of the condition of each trap.

The heads should not be 'in use' during this time.

"Why is the door on that head shut?" asked the duty pig.

"I don't know sir," Buster answered honestly, frowning and shaking his head. He swore the heads were empty before he readied himself for rounds.

The duty officer pushed the offending doors open with the tip of his shoe.

Sitting, polishing his todger was an MEM, grunting and as he drew breath as he was reaching his vinegar strokes.

With myself, the duty pig and three other lads about to crack up, the officer said:

"Excellent wrist action son."

We all moved on, leaving the said MEM to his activity.

Work up

Gen

This was during the mid-1970's, aboard HMS VALIANT at Faslane. (Ready for work up.)

Nice CSST staff warn a possible evolution may be running diesels, a fuel pipe fracture and fire in the hydraulic plant.

At sea couple of days later, we were ordered to run both diesels.
A few minutes later, our TG Tiff comes up in his broadest Yorkshire accent "Maneuvering-TG."

"Maneuvering."

"Feckin' diesel pipes fractured, fecking oil pissin' all oer t'shop, fecking hydraulic pumps just caught fire.

Oh, bollocks, fecking switchboard's just gone up in smoke, Mudguard, Lifeguard, Safeguard or whatever the feck it is, I got a fucking fire on my hands down here."

Despite the screams of mirth, the fire was rapidly extinguished.

Heads up

Here are a few things you should know before joining the Royal Navy.

The Duty watch does not require a key from stores.

The Liberty Boat does not require a pair of oars.

Paint does not come in Tartan.

You cannot collect steam in a bucket.

Black ham does not come in a tin.

A long weight requires a long wait.

Skyhooks are not military issue.

Never ask about the golden rivet.

A dose is not a measurement.

<<< >>>

One of the best wind-ups I witnessed was onboard HMS Ardent.
A chief stoker sent a junior MEM to get some air hose from stores.

The junior returned sometime later with three Mars Bars.

The Chief, using a string of expletives asks why the fuck he was being given three bars of nutty.

The Junior MEM replied, "The NAFFI didn't have any 'Areo's', so I got Mars Bars instead."

A Stokers confession

Dit

While based at an un-nameable establishment, my mates and I found a way into the beer cellar.

It was under the bar, via an old, forgotten dumbwaiter.

Late at night, when there were fewer bodies around, we would acquire a case or two, bringing them up from the dark cellar by the said dumbwaiter.

Luckily, our mess had a 'loft' style hatch in the ceiling, giving access to an area large enough to hold several cases of beer.

We had a great little business going, selling cheap cans to Jack and over the road to the Jennies in their block.

Until we all got drafted.

I found myself on the Blake, where I heard that a refurbishment was underway at a certain shore establishment, where there were questions being asked about a random quantity of beer found in one of the mess's roof voids.

I kept schtum, as I knew nothing of it, of course.

A watch, some beers and a Dgħajsa

Gen

M alta, Valletta.

Pissed, returning to ship and making our way to the dghajsa's in the Grand Harbour when we spotted a bar which was still open

We all agreed that it would be best if we supped one more drink before going back to the ship.

The problem was, no one had any Klebies left, so it was agreed we would pawn B. C's watch.

He objected, but to no avail.

The Barman agreed to take and hold the watch for seven days. After which time if we had not settled the bill he would be free to sell the watch and recoup his earning by doing so.

The barman served us all a cold beer.

After which we set off to the harbour to get the aforementioned dghajsa out to the ship.

B.C. was whinging about his expensive and valuable watch he was certain he would never see again.

On hearing a loud splash, I turned about and looked at the water behind me.

B.C. it seemed, in his pissed and angry state, decided to swim back to the ship

I shrugged, along with everyone else and clambered into the rocking dghajsa.

B.C. eventually got back and, once he was dry, continued to whinge about his effing watch.

He was right though. He never saw his watch again as we sailed off in the early hours of the following morning.

We did have a bit of a whip around and set him up with a new 'Seiko' when we reached Honky Fid.

After all, three months of B.C.'s constant dripping was enough to turn us all into frigging psychopaths.

Jack and Miss World...

Joke

A...re shipwrecked and end up on a desert island.

They make themselves a mud hut, one each, at either end of the island but agree to meet up at the palm tree in the centre of the island every Saturday night, for a run ashore.

After a few months, they both get a bit carried away and they do the deed.

Afterwards, while they are lying under the stars enjoying a blueliner, Jack leans across and says, "That was fantastic... but could you do me a favour?"

"Of course, Jack," says Miss World, "after that, I would do anything, what have you got in mind?"

"Well," says Jack, I know we don't meet up on a Sunday lunchtime, but could we meet up at the palm tree tomorrow?"

"OK," says Miss World.

"And," says Jack, could you please wear these No 8s (*AWD for newbies*)."

A little surprised, she agrees and they go their separate ways, back to their own huts.

Sunday lunchtime comes around.

Jack walks up to the Palm Tree and meets up with Miss World wearing the No 8s.

"Hello mate," says Jack, "You'll never guess who I shagged last night.................."

An incident on the Eagle

Gen? Circa 1970

T he 984 Radar watchkeepers were housed in gangway mess 3R2.

I was one of the fortunate during this particular 'Flying Stations', as I was off watch, fucking about in the Mess.

The SRE (*Ship's Radio Equipment*) broadcast, announced Flying Stations were finishing just as the last Buccaneer was coming in.

Thing is as it landed, it slipped a 500-pound bomb, leaving it stranded on the flight deck, just above 'R' section.

The bomb, the SRE broadcast announced, was live. *"But as the impact from 'falling off' the Buccaneer and hitting the deck had not set it off, it 'should be' safe, until it could be defused."*

Now, Jack being Jack, our reaction was to make a few comments about 'Airy Fairies' being a bunch of wankers, (and so forth.)

A few moments later, one of the REM's mentioned the bomb, which was immediately above our heads. *"Did we realise there were only two decks separating us, from the offending item?"* he asked.

The discussions then focused on what the destructive power of a 500-pound bomb could be and what it could do regarding the strength of an armoured flight deck.

We were simply a bunch of young Greenies, we had no idea and no facts but suddenly it seems the whole mess held 'expert opinions' and piped-up for this in-depth discussion.

It was agreed, if the bomb went off, we would not have a much of an issue, excepting maybe a pounding headache.

However, within ten minutes the entire mess seemed to fade out. So many people suddenly needed the heads, or to go and see an oppo, or remembered they were wanted at the far end of the ship.

Even more unusually, those who wanted to go to the heads went to the heads.

Once it was announced the bomb was 'made safe' the mess started to fill again.

The topic of conversation that evening revealed that keeping a stiff upper lip can cause a weak bladder, something I never knew before that day.

Gibraltar

Back in the 20th Century

On a sludgemarine.

Taking a baby RO(SM)'s out for a *'bit of a run ashore'*.

It was his first time on the Rock, so he needed a guided tour of Gib's Pubs, Clubs and Fish, chip and chicken shops.

The evening wore on and young Scotty, now pissed as a fart, was getting a bit bolshy.

Scotty was, when wet through, at least seven stone of weak piss. So, when he offered the gorilla-like 'doorman' from one of the clubs, out for a round of fisticuffs. I knew it was time to take him back to the boat.

One the way back, Scotty puked over his feet. The stench of his spew affecting me in some strange way I decided he should learn the noble art of 'Car Walking'.

For those not familiar with this ancient skill, it is the ability to run up the back of the car, over its roof, down the front to the end of the bonnet, where you either jump to the road or leap to the next parked car and repeat the exercise. The further you get without touching the road the better you have done.

After watching me demonstrate this art, Scotty had to have a go himself and fell through the soft top sunroof of a little sports car.

I forgot to mention for him to watch out for cabriolets and cars with those soft pram roofs. After this episode, I was fcd up with babysitting, so I stuffed Scotty into a taxi and sent him back.

For me, an old seasoned hand, the night was still young, so I popped into Six Steps Down for a quick sherbet or two,

Once I had healthy gibber on and the barmaid began to look reasonably pretty I called it a night and headed back while I could still stand (partially) upright.

As usual, we were in one of those little shite hole hotels. I grabbed my room key from the Gibbo on reception and fucked off to the lift, up to the room.

When I got to the room the door was wide open and Scotty was nowhere to be seen. As his pit was undisturbed, I got a tad concerned.

There was loud snoring coming from the next room, which door was also wide open and I could see Scotty crashed out on some fucker's pit.

I levered the drunken Scotty from the bed and dumped him on his own pit.

In the time it took me to 'rescue' Scotty, some thieving twat had done our room over. My new denim jacket, with about £70 quid in the pocket, had gone walkies.

I picked up the room phone and dialled reception, to report the suspected burglary.

I let the phone ring for an age before I lost the plot and started to wobble.
Partly because I was pissed and partly with the adrenalin rush from being so fucking angry.

I bumbled out of the room and took the lift to the ground floor.

When I Arrived at reception, I was still yelling into the 'phone, which I still had clenched in my hand, trailing several feet of cable and some loose plaster.

"I'VE BEEN RINGING THIS BASTARD PHONE FOR FIFTEEN FUCKING MINUTES.
I'VE JUST BEEN FUCKING ROBBED." I shouted in frustration.

Then seemed to do the trick, the receptionist took some notice of me at last and made a phone call to the police.

The Gibraltar Crusher Division arrived and immediately arrested me for damage to the hotel's property.
I complained, explaining I called THEM to report a robbery.

Ramming my arms up my back until my shoulder blades popped, we all took a nice stroll to the hotel room.

Scotty, seeing two Killick Regulators, sprang out of his drunken stupor and started to throw shoes, light fittings and the kettle at my escorts.

Which got him arrested too.
That was when Gibraltar CID turned up, demanding we get turned over to there custody.

The room I found Scotty Crashed out in was occupied by two mingers from Tangiers who, on finding the hotel room doors open, accused us of breaking into their room and stealing a load of 'jewellery'.

The RN crushers lost the argument, so young Scotty and I ended up in the Central Police station. It was two days and nights before our D.O. got us out.

We were both confined to the boat for the rest of the visit.
So, Scotty got his first run ashore in Gib, one he swears he will never forget.

I bloody love Gibraltar!

Wind up

Gen

Alongside in Dolphin, on a quiet Sunday.

The best way to relieve the boredom, it was decided, was to wind-up the Ark Royal, which was in drydock in Pompey.

A telephone call was made to the bosun's mate, allegedly from the Queens Harbour Master's office, enquiring as to the depth of water in the bottom of the dry dock.

"I don't know sir," was the reply to our question.

"Well, go and find out," was the curt response.

About 30 minutes later, a puffing bosuns mate *(who'd obviously just completed the marathon of going into the dock bottom and then back up to the gangway)*, came back to the phone.

"About 3 inches, sir," he puffed.

"Very good - pipe hands to bathe,"

Pissed ourselves laughing.

Policeman's Knock

Joke

A policeman knocked on my door and showed me a picture of my wife.

He said, 'I'm afraid, it looks like she's been hit by a bus.'

I said, 'I know, but she's good with the kids.'

<<<< >>>>

The Blond & the Beer

Joke

Yesterday morning I bought two six-pack of Corona beer on sale at the liquor store. I placed them on the front seat of the car and headed home.

I stopped at the gas station where a gorgeous drop-dead almost blonde was filling up her car at the next pump. It was very warm and she was wearing tight shorts and a light top which was wide open.

She glanced at the beer, bent over and knocked on my passenger window.

She said, in a sexy voice, "I'm a big believer in barter, mister. Would you be interested in trading sex for beer?"

I thought for a few seconds and asked, "What kind of beer you got?"

Meeting Joe Morrow

I can't remember the exact year, but think it was 1968.

We were on exercise with the Yanks and Cannooks, on the Oracle

Only one of the big ends went and we diverted to Halifax, Nova-Scotia, to strip the engine and undertake repairs.

Back then the bars closed at 2200, but Jack being Jack, we found the naughty places.

One was downstairs under a Chinese restaurant. If you had a meal, you could stay as long as you wanted. You had to ask for a *'pot of tea for two'* and wink at the waiter.

The sight of thirty hairy arsed, unwashed, stubble wearing submariners, sitting around tables, ordering tea and winking at waiters, was something to behold, I can tell you.

We found a nightclub where an American comedian called Joe Morrow was performing.

Somehow, we found our way to the dressing rooms and befriended Joe Morrow, who agreed to pop down to the boat at tot time the following day. Which he did.

Joe listened to our dits and moans about our skipper, a certain Lt cdr John Coward.

He left late that day, after a little kip and promised he would send a tape of his next radio show, once he got back home.

A month or so later we received the tape and a LRO asked for it to be broadcast on the boat's Tannoy.

After a few jokes, Joe Morrow referred to 'his friends' on the 'British submarine the Oracle'.

Joe continued by saying, he was forwarding "a parcel of two bits of wood, one 2 cubits x 6 cubits and another 12 cubits by 2 cubits, 4 nails and a crown of thorns, so the crew could crucify your skipper John Coward."

Funnily enough, the tannoy system went dead almost immediately and the tape was never seen again.

The port donk was stripped, the bearing required was identified.
At that time, Faslane was undergoing modernisation and all requests for spares needed to be identified by part numbers, not names. The part number was found, a signal sent to Faslane.

The part was then dispatched from Faslane to Edinburgh airport by courier, flown to Halifax, picked up by another courier at the airport and transported directly to the engine room.

The package was opened to reveal a nice shiny tin of cleaning paste.

Aladdin's lamp Song

Ditty

There was a lad called Aladdin, who had a magic lamp.
He stole it off a matelot, who was fathoms up a tramp.
He stole it from a matelot to see what he could get,
and he rubbed and he rubbed and he ain't got fuck all yet.
Oh! Fah, lah, le lah, lah le dee, sixteen anners and one rupee
feed of arse up a sycamore tree, oh bugger Janner.

Now, the Sultan said to Aladdin, my palace you will paint.
Aladdin, like a big O.D., said no I fucking ain't.
So off he went, with a one-inch brush and a pot of black
enamel,
and he shoved it up the arsehole of the Sultans favourite
camel.
Oh! Fah, lah, le lah, lah le dee, sixteen anners one rupee
feed of arse on a sycamore tree oh bugger Janner.

You make farce, kiss my arse, make fast the dingy.
You make farce, kiss my arse, make fast the dingy,
and we'll all go back to oggie land, to oggie land,
and we'll all go back to oggie land, where they can't tell
paper, from tissue paper, tissue paper, marmalade or jam.
Oggie, oggie, oggie, oye, oye, oye!
Oggie, oggie, oggie, oye, oye, oye!

Penang, mobies & jet skis

Dit

P enang, Malaysia.

As soon as you step outside the dockyard, you find entire streets full of motorbike rental shops. Obviously, the first thing we did was get ourselves some transport.

It is complete luck of the draw what you get, anything from the latest rev and go moped to Chinese copies of Harleys.

I ended up with a Honda something or other, not that the badges on the machines meant much, they all looked the same.

The bloke was writing out my form, he said "name?'

I replied "Chris..." before I could give my surname, he cut me off and said, "OK Mr. Chris, what hotel you stay?"

I gave him the name of the first place I'd seen outside the dockyard and he handed me the keys.

That was it, no ID, no proof, nothing.

Of course, we decided to ride carefully, in convoy and relatively slowly; because they were unfamiliar roads and not in the best of upkeep.

Like fuck we did.
We raced each other to the nearest beach like the bunch of twats we were. *(The beach was subsequently destroyed by a Tsunami a few months later by the way.)*

The beach was mega, about 2 miles long, filled with 5-star hotels, bars and blokes renting jet skis.

We found a spot with a bar and an extensive cocktail menu. It had a 2 for 1 happy hour deal which lasted all day. Big eats... oh, yeah, we feasted on lobster and other seafood, some totally unrecognisable, but delicious.

We got smashed out of our heads on daiquiris.

Me and my oppo, Smokey, rented a jet ski. The bloke said, *"half an hour, stay within view of the beach."*

We took the skis as far out to sea as you could go without shitting yourself. The beach was indistinguishable from the rest of the land mass.

The only way we found our way back was because we could see people on parachutes attached to speedboats, otherwise, we would have been fucked.

We followed a Gucci as fuck looking superyacht and did some jumps in its wake.

I fell off, vomited everywhere, too many daiquiris I guess? When we eventually returned to the beach, some hours later, the jet ski man was threaders, we had truly taken the piss.

The rest of that day is all a misty blur.

But, I am told, it was a great run!

The Firing Line

Falklands war, Gen Dit, No. 1

Picture the scene; we are in the Falklands Sound. It is 06:30 on May 19th, 1982.

As usual, it is a cold, damp misty morning.

We are ready to give support bombardment against reported Argentinean troop movement, somewhere ashore.

The weather closing in and visibility is down to about a mile. The SAS spotters have long gone to find a warm cup of Khai and some scran.

Argent slowly creeps along the coast. Inside all eyes are glued to the radar screens. Outside eyes are prying through many pairs of binoculars.

A call from a lookout:

"TROOP MOVEMENT. RED 110, RANGE. 6 MILES".

All lookouts rush over to the port side, a gap in the mist reveals about eight heavily armed units heading down the hillside.

The Skipper asked the army Colonel, who was assigned to be liaison between us and the friendly SAS troops ashore.

"Who do those units belong to?"

The Colonel studied his map for, trying to match any intelligence.

After what seemed like an age, he said, "No reported designated friendly troops, gathered or collected, within the assigned point specified area."

"Do you mean, they are not ours?" asked the skipper.

Orders were given. "ENGAGE THE ENEMY."

The gunnery officer ordered,

"FOUR FIVES (four & a half inch guns) STAND TOO. POLICY SHORE BOMBARDMENT. LOOKOUT BEARING RED 085, ELEVATION 40, THREE ROUNDS FOR EFFECT FIRE."
Boom, boom, boom.

The shells landed accurately amongst the convoy on the slopes. Who started to make their escape, moving haphazardly in all directions.

The guns fired a second salvo.

We cheered the shells landing, our nostril full of the smell of cordite.
About 30 shells landed before the movement ashore ceased.

We cautiously approached the shore for observation and confirmation with cameras rolling, ready to beam the information back to MOD in the UK.

A lookout on then started to piss himself laughing.

"GREAT SHOOTING," he said, "WE HAVE SCORED OUR FIRST KILL. FIVE COWS AND TWO SHEEP".

The cameras clicked off and we quietly slipped out of the sound.

<<< >>>

Stopped by the Rozzer's

Joke

I was stopped by the police around 2 am this morning. The officer asked me where I was going at that time.

I replied, "I'm on my way to a lecture about alcohol abuse and the effects it has on the human body, as well as the dangers of smoking and staying out late"

The officer replied, " Oh really........ and who is giving that lecture at this time of night?"

"My wife"

All that Glisters

My first sea-going ship was HMS Battleaxe.

Not the posh Type 22 of the same name, but the old Weapon Class Radar Picket, with open bridge and hammocks.

I joined the Battleaxe at Invergordon in the middle of winter. Just as she set sail, into a force 9. You can say my first-day at sea was unforgettable.
However, my first run ashore was Aberdeen, my hometown.

Now, way back in the days before black gold was found offshore, Aberdeen was a busy fishing port, in fact, the busiest and biggest in the UK.

The nightlife was more akin to Bangkok or Hong Kong as many bars around the docks were frequented by ladies of ill-repute or lose morals or both.

Before leaving the ship, we were all advised which establishments it was best not to frequent.

We then made a bee-line for those, as if they were recommended.

Note that 'runs ashore' were always in uniform in those days.

Before we ventured ashore, another warning was one about the possibility of catching 'anti-social' diseases, from those ladies, in those bars, we were advised not to frequent.

Our attention was also drawn to the location of the condom drawer, under the Sick Bay hatch.

While the Battleaxe was *'showing the flag'*, the Lady Provost of Aberdeen, plus an entourage which included the Skipper, the Jimmy, and a whole bunch of civvy knobs were doing an official tour of the ship.

The good Lady Provost stopped outside the Sick Bay and asked, "What do you hide in here?" as she pulled open the condom drawer.

She tugged it open with such force it slipped off the runners spilling a pile of foil-wrapped packages over her shoes.

"Ah", she said, "Barley Sugar, what a good idea for your long journeys."

Luckily, she did not have a sweet tooth.

A wheely true tale

Gash Dit

One steward said he was sunbathing below the ski-ramp on a carrier when one of the Sea Harriers took off.

The roaring above the steward's head made him glance upwards. Which was fortunate, because, falling from the sky above his bronzing position, was the wheel from the Jump Jet.

The steward boasts he caught the wheel and waltzed up to the flight deck, handing it to the senior WAFU saying, "I believe this is yours."

Anyone wanting to claim this dit as their own, hands up?

An ex-Jack's dit

From when working as a civvy.

But I thought it deserved an outing here because we can all relate.

'EX RN'

Some years ago. I was working for a distribution company as an electrician.

The company invested millions on a fully-automated conveyor system for their main centre.

After installation, everything ran smoothly, at least for a day, and then it happened.

Everything stopped dead. It packed up working without warning.

We poked about in all the control panels checking for broken wires, blown fuses, burnt out relays, suspect component boards, in fact, anything which might suggest what or where the problem lay.

We could find nothing untoward. In desperation, the company sent for an engineer form the German company who installed the apparatus.

The German engineer stood in front of the main control panel with a deepening frown forming on his face and much scratching of his head as he contemplated the issue.

Without warning the system burst into life again.

Neither the engineer or I had touched a single component.

I asked, "fucking hell Hans, now what do we do?"

"I tell you vot vee do," he replied, "vee close zee fucking door and vee valk avay."

Luck has it, the system ran smoothly, without issue, from that time on.

Weight Loss

Joke

An overweight matelot was ordered to lose weight before being considered for a leadership course or face medical discharge from the mob.

Reading the Navy News, he came across an advert saying, "Lose 10lb in just one week."

He walked to the phone box, just outside Pompey dockyard gates and rang the advertisers, "I would like to lose 10lb in one week" he said.

"No problem," said the voice at the other end, "be ready tomorrow at 06:00 Hrs. But remember,

Jack was dutifully standing by his front door at 06:00 hrs. as requested.
When the doorbell rang he opened the door, expecting a delivery man with a large box of fitness equipment, only to find a red-hot babe wearing nothing but suspenders and lacy underwear.

She say's to Jack, "If you can catch me, you can make mad passionate love to me". With that, the girl turns and runs up the street.
Jack starts after her, but soon the rum and fags have him panting and wheezing. There was no way he could catch her.
Each morning, for an entire week the girl arrived at his house dead on 06:00 Hrs. Jack never caught her, but he did lose the 10lbs he wanted.

Jack 'phones the company again, this time asking for the program designed to lose him 20lb.

"Of course, but remember the rules; whatever happens, you have to complete the whole week".

"Yep, I know," said Jack.

The next morning, at exactly 06:00 the doorbell rings. Jack opens it to find the girl of his dreams standing there, she was as naked as a Jaybird.

"If you catch me, you can do anything you want with me," she says, starting to run away from him. Jack gave chase.

He even gave up the blueliners and the Pusser's Rum and, by the end of the week, has lost the full 20lbs, but he had not caught the girl, yet.

Fancying his chances, as the new non-drinking, non-smoking, lightweight version of his former self, Jack called the company once more and requested they enrol him on the 'lose 50lb' course.

"Are you sure?" asked the voice on the phone, "It's a tough challenge and you cannot back out once you start, you have to complete the entire week.".

Jack said he was more than ready for the challenge.
Dead on 06:00 he opens the door expecting to see a wonderful naked woman, but finds a huge naked Royal Marine, wearing nothing but his green beret.

The Marine says to Jack, "start running because if I catch you, I'm going to fuck you"

Doha, Oh dear!

Gen Dit

Walking through Doha airport, towards my departure gate, when an attractive African lady smiles at me and asks if I want a whore.

"No thanks," I say, "I am a married man".

She looked at me strangely, even a little confused.

I kept walking and soon passed a sign which said, "Lahore"

What a Muppet.

The Bridge Run

Falklands War, Gen Dit, No.2

It was another cold and damp morning in the South Atlantic Ocean during May 1982.

W e are a group of ships steaming off the Falklands, waiting for the *'morning run'* of Argentinean planes

After several days their morning presence becomes monotonous.

This day was just another normal day at sea.

I was on the bridge, which was full of 'gofers', so they can run down the mess with an early dit, the "you'll never guess," or "I just saw." Type of shit.

Also, on the bridge is the Skipper, the OOW, Navigator, a Midshipman and a bunch of others who are on duty.

On the port wing, staring out of a pair of binoculars, looking for anything and trying to look important, is a PO Yeoman.

The Buffer and says to him in a low voice "What you looking at?"

"Without taking his eyes from the lens, the Yeoman says, "Nothing', it's too quiet this morning. I got a feeling it will be a quiet day."

The Buffer picks up a pair of binoculars and, standing quietly next to him stares out of the window too.

A shout from the gun lookout above.

"RED 090 FAR AND LOW, TWO AIRCRAFT, SLOW MOVEMENT."

All eyes run over to the place where the Yeoman and the Buffer are stood.

Seconds tick by as all try and focus their bins. Then someone shouts,
"GOT 'EM, RED 90, TWO SMALL DOTS OVER THE HORIZON."

One by one the voices pipe-up, "I see them," "They look small," and "Gootum."

The Buffer says casually "They look almost stationary, not moving, just getting a bit bigger. I wonder what poor bugger they are going for."

The Yeoman replies, "No idea Buffs, let's take a look."

With that, the duo walk over to the other side of the bridge put their binoculars up to their eyes again and scan the sea.

It is an empty void.

Together they say, *"shit, they're coming for us."*

The bridge comes alive as orders are shouted.

Immediately below the bridge is the Operations Room, full of radar, sonar and missilemen, manning headsets and staring into brightly lit screens in a dark and quiet environment.

Someone said, "Why do we need all this equipment. If we want to know where the enemy is, just get them above to do a bridge run."

Ode, from a Jenny

Since I was just a little girl, I've always hoped to be
A sailor on a frigate, a` sailing out at sea.
So, when at last I hit the street and had to get a job
I signed up on the dotted line and soon was in the mob.

At first, I didn't like it, and I wanted out.
'Cos the Chief GI had attitude and all he did was shout.
But later as I settled in, it didn't seem so bad
So, I thought I`d stay awhile, and later I was glad.

The kit was bloody awful, it wasn't me at all
There was nothing in my kit bag that made my bum look small
I looked just like a scran bag, all dressed up like my Nan.
And when I wore my No 1`s, I was looking like a man.

So, first job was to get to grips, with this ill-fitting kit
And with a crafty nip and tuck, I soon got it to fit.
Then out on the parade ground, the feeling it was grand
To march along with head held high, behind a bootneck band.

With Raleigh done and dusted, my training at an end
I headed off to my first ship, with all my newfound friends
We were the first to serve at sea, down in the jenny's mess
Though I suspect we weren't the first who liked to wear a
dress.

The captain welcomed us aboard, whilst staring at our tits

and showed us round our new mess deck, we were the only splits,
just six of us in one small mess, it was more like a pen
but no one asked if we'd prefer, to rough it with the men.

Clear lower deck, the QM piped, get fell in up top
Line up for leaving harbour, and that includes you lot
But as we slipped and headed out, I knew I'd rather be
Taking in the shopping, there at Gun Wharf Quay.

Turning down the channel, and heading for the Med.
With some on watch or turned to, we took to our beds
Two days out with no let up, and some started to moan
If he can't stop us wobbling, then I'm going home

But we weren't really bothered; we took it in our stride
And anyway, when you're at sea, there is no place to hide.
Way down in the jenny's mess, we didn't mind rough weather
We all sat in the corner and hugged and cried together.

Soon the rock appeared ahead, as Gib came into view
We'd never seen the place before, to us, it was all new.
"We wanna see the rock apes", we all said with a cheer.
Then stay on board the buffer said, there's plenty of 'em here.

Loaded up with rabbits and looking for a ride
Come in my bar said a voice, all your mates are inside
Through the doorway in the gloom, we thought he must be wrong

Then we heard a stoker belting out a song

Welcomed to the table, soon we all joined in
Our singing voices all improved, as we had more gin
Three hours later we were drunk, but we still were able
To show the lads a highland reel and not fall off the table.

Jacks repertoire went on and on, it was all new to me,
I laughed until the tears rolled down, and I couldn't see
Still dancing when the clock struck four, we had had enough
So, we got a `fast black` back on board, so we could sleep it off

Arriving at the gangway, and twittering like a bird
We told the quartermaster all that we had heard
Gibbering like idiots we propositioned him
Yes. Yes. he said, perhaps next, now go and get turned in.

Back at sea and heading home, the Biscay waves were kind
And soon we`d left the sunshine, a long way far behind
The attitude on board the ship, was different and we knew
That we had been accepted now, as members of the crew.

I've had some strange reactions and sometimes just blank
stares
Now working shoulder to shoulder with the men, no one really
cares
I've served my queen on land and sea for 15 years and more
But I'll never forget that night in Gib and my first run ashore.

Dizzy-fit

Gen Dit

"QUIS ERIPIET DENTES"
(WHO WILL DRAW MY TEETH?)

I cannot reveal the identity of the main character in this

dit, so I shall call him Simon 'Axe' Bigbones, for want of a better name. Because if I called him *'Chopper'* it might give the game away.

'Axe' was under pun's, 9's, for some forgotten reason; but was granted leave to play rugby for the ships team, against the Foreign Legion, in Dakar. (1977).

I have no recollection of how the game went, or who won, excepting to say the legionnaires were a bunch of very large, tough, handy fellows.

However, a condition of Axe's leave to play for the ship's company was he must wear rig. Full blues, no.2's when travelling to and from the rugby playing fields.

It was a condition set by the Joss, who was not too pleased with the granting of Axe's leave whilst he was under pun's.

Now, Axe being Axe, the Josses orders seemed to have slipped his memory, because, after the game. Axe decided to swap his rig with a legionnaire.

You can, with little imagination, picture the Joss man having a dizzy-fit as Axe returned, walking up the gangplank looking like fucking Beau Geste without his camel.

Oh, how we laughed!

Good old days and a lot of fun, though.

Original Navy sayings... *(part 3)*

No room to swing a cat

Referred to a small space or crowded area, if it was not large enough to swing the whip, (*the Cat'o nine tails*).

Over a barrel

Sailors were often strapped over a barrel before being flogged.

Longshot

The term refers to firing a canon beyond its range, knowing it had little chance of success.

Piping hot

The bo'sun would blow on a pipe to tell mess masters food was ready and to go and collect it while still hot.

Square meal

A sailor's plate or tray was a wooden square. This wooden board also lent itself to the word board, in the term 'Bed and Board' used for lodging houses.

Tommy's Out

I was told this by a Stoker.

I am sure this is a Gen Dit, as it holds echoes of a stoker's game called 'Splat'. In fact, this one is so fucked up, I want to believe it's not true.

A few years ago, some fine young matelots from HMS Tiger introduced me to a game they called **'Tommy's Out'**.

This game is very much like a childhood game of 'Hide and Seek', but... with two major differences.

Firstly, it only takes one person to decide to play Tommy's Out. After which everyone else **must** play, by default.

Secondly, with 'Tommy's Out' you do not 'Seek' another person, you 'Seek' a freshly laid turd. The 'Tommy' which has just come 'out'.

Generally, the game is played when visiting, or as an invited guest, at someone's home.

Most often during a booze-fueled party.

The person initiating the game, the one who has just 'Hidden Tommy', walks into the room where the host and most guests are and announces in a loud voice that,

"TOMMY'S OUT"

(Sometimes, there are a few punches thrown in anger or disbelief.
The Tommy layer has also been known to be forcefully ejected on occasion.)

After which the hosts and guests have little option but to set out to find where 'Tommy' is hiding.

This game has continued for several years and people have been getting rather inventive and ingenious, regarding places to hide Tommy.

This is where my Stoker mate cannot help chuckling as he continues this dit, which has now cost me three pints of Badgers Best to hear!

It was, he says, a hot summer June day when this game of 'Tommy's Out', one which was started about one month earlier, came to an end.

The game began when the initiator decided it would be an excellent idea to hide Tommy a low-fat soya spread tub, which alone would have been a well thought, secretive hiding place for Tommy.

Now, to give this person their due. (*I am not at liberty to disclose which gender she is*), was a little more cunning...

Before placing Tommy in the low-fat soya tub, they removed the butter-like spread, placed Tommy carefully in the base of the plastic container, then replaced the original content, putting Tommy snugly to bed in the process.

Needless to say, no one could find Tommy during the original hunt. Some even suggested the whole thing was little more than a hoax.

Now we must travel forward, to that sunny day in June I mentioned earlier.

The residents of the said house were once again hosting a social gathering.
This time, it was the wife's parents visiting for a long weekend.

To make the most of such, they had arisen early and were busily preparing breakfast for the family before setting off for a 'day out'.

Mother, using the low-fat soya spread to butter the fourth round of toast, uncovered Tommy who was still lingering in the base of the tub.

With the realisation there was only the thinnest of spread covering Tommy, the rest of it being used during the preceding month did not bode well for a feeling of wellbeing or lend itself to a harmonious and happy weekend with the in-laws as planned.

Now, sit back and take a little time to digest this tale... well, perhaps digest is not a favourable word considering.

A dit, well worth the price of three pints, me thinks.

A Few Quickies

Jokes

Did you hear about the fat, alcoholic transvestite - All he wanted to do was eat, drink and be Mary.

I got invited to a party and was told to dress to kill. Apparently, a turban, beard and a backpack wasn't what they had in mind.

After a night of drink, drugs and wild sex, Jim woke up to find himself next to a really ugly woman. That's when he realised he had made it home safely.

Paddy says to Mick, "Christmas is on Friday this year". Mick said, "Let's hope it's not the 13th then."

My mate just hired an Eastern European cleaner, took her 15 hours to hoover the house. Turns out she was a Slovak.

Since the snow came all the wife has done is look through the window. If it gets any worse, I'll have to let her in.

Arriving in Bangkok

Gen Dit

We sailed up a massive river, I forget its name, gradually moving inland, where the water became dirtier. There was a ton of gash and dead dogs floating about.

At one point we passed the pride of the Thai Navy. I was instructed to pipe the still as we went past.

I looked everywhere for a shiny ship, then I noticed a Thai Admiral standing on the open bridge of some rusty grey shit heap.

I piped the still in salute.

Eventually, we docked in Bangkok. A spare tug needed to move a ton of rotting gash away from the jetty, so we could get alongside.

I recall a local dive team turning up in a tuk-tuk.

They arrived to cut some fishing net off our hull which had become snagged around the LOG reader (*basically the ship's speedo*) as we came up that shit creek.

I watched with amazement as one of these local divers stripped down to his kegs, stuck a garden hose into his mouth and jumped in the amongst all the floating shite, moving a few animal carcasses and sharp needle aside as he cleared a gap, so he could dive down.

He had a huge knife clenched between his teeth, pink goggles and yellow kegs, which could have been budgie smuggler speedos.

Attached to the other end of the garden hose the diver had in his mouth, was another skinny local lad, who was pumping away with a car foot pump as if he was inflating a tyre.

Welcome to Thailand, 1969.

I am unsure if anything's changed since then, I have never been back.

Box of frogs

Gash Dit?

Andy, a WAFU, returned late one night.

He had some black crap smeared down one leg of his trousers, he was bloody, bruised and adrift.

But he was laughing his head off.

We were in France and Andy was on a regular run ashore when he got parted from his oppos. But, as you do, Andy continued to down the bevvies.

A few too many Pastis 55's and not enough water caused him to upset some local froggies who waited outside the bar, where they gave pissed up Andy a good old kicking the moment he left the bar.

As pissed as he was Andy knew he was defenceless, so did the next best thing and curled up into a ball, hoping they would not do too much damage and give up quickly.

As he lay there he pleaded for mercy, "Mercy, mercy, mercy" he shouted.

Now, the local lads think he is one sandwich short of a picnic and, after one last half-hearted kick, leg it before the local gendarme arrive.

As Andy is laying on the deck listening to them running off he realizes what 'Mercy' means in French.

This is what he was still laughing about as he clambered up the gangway that night/early morning.

C'est la vie.

As they say somewhere frogish.

Ex Jack, and a trip to Weston

Joke

It began a week ago, the day my wife and I spent a day in Weston-Super-Mare.

As is with our unpredictable British summer, it was bloody freezing and blowing a frigging gale, but we were determined to enjoy ourselves, whatever.

We got into Weston abound half-ten in the morning and were ready for a bit of scran and a good old cuppa.

Eventually, we came across a café. I think all the staff were some sort of refugees by the way they spoke.

We ordered 2 x full English breakfasts and a pot of English breakfast tea.
Feeling brave, and as this was our 'Nice day out', we decided to dine al fresco and took a pew on the street where we could, watch the world go by as we ate.

There was another table directly in front of us, at which sat four people.

Now, these four diners were, how shall I put this... not a quite a full box of matches. In fact, they were more like an empty tool-box.

The minibus they arrived in was parked on the double yellows, with a 'blue badge' in the window. Painted on the side was the slogan *'Llandudno Window Lickers World Tour'* emblazoned on the side.

Their carer's arrived, bringing trays of food for the four.
The wife and I set about own breakfasts, but I could not draw my eyes away from the other table.

Fortunately, they were seated directly behind my wife, so I could look without it being obvious.

It was then I saw Florence.

I knew her name because it was written in brightly coloured wax crayon on a piece of paper stapled to her 'I love Skegness' baseball cap.

Florence was deep in conversation with the other three members of her group, who were struggling to take the corks off the end of their forks, whilst rocking backwards and forwards in a somewhat rhythmic motion.

"MmmmmmmmmmlllllllllllllllllllaaaaRRRRrrrrrrrrrrggghhhhhh", said Florence.

This upset one of her fellow diners. Who finally managed to pull the cork from the end of his fork, but lost control of his arm in the process, resulting in him stabbing himself in the cheek.

Finding this rather amusing, the others started to jab their own forks into his ears.

A bit of attention from one if the carver's and everything settled down.

I watched as Florence daintily set about demolishing her scran. I am uncertain if it was the way baked-bean juice dribbled over her multiple chins, the steaming globules of porridge she managed to stick to her eye-lids or the greasy chunks of black pudding protruding from her nostrils.

But when she looked at me, pointing with an egg yolk smothered finger and screamed.
"EEEEEEEEEeeeeeeeeeeeeeeeeeeeeeeeeeeeeeeeeeeeeMMIIIaarrrrr rrrrr".
allowing her half-masticated sausage to tumble from her open mouth and slide into the lap of her power rangers shell suite, I shall never know, but from then on, I only had eyes for Florence.

I was almost oblivious to her friends, as they poured hot drinking chocolate into their eyes.

Florence looked like she had climbed out of a skip of Union Street Kebab shop.

I was about to say something when the carer herded them back to the minibus.

As the mini-bus drove away, my last sight of Florence was of her staring out of the rear window, drawing patterns on the glass with a half-sausage and a handful of luke-warm fried tomatoes.

I am now desperately trying to find this lost love, who was taken away after such a short time.

I have tried various Social Networking Portals like www.Spakkers-Reunited.co.uk, www.DribblingFaceBook.com and www.indowlickers.net

But sadly, to no avail.

I shall go mad and die of a broken heart if I cannot find my 22 stone, 3 feet 5-inch-tall, ginger-haired soul mate.

Can you help?

She was driven away in a Toyota Granvia, 3 litre MPV.

I need to find it because I want the head gasket and radiator, so I can repair my own piece of Japanese shite before the 12th January, when I have to drive my wife to Southampton.

In Rio

Gen

We were joined by a group of US Coast Guards, many who lived in our mess.

They were exactly how yank soldiers and marines are portrayed in films, gung-ho attitude, built like brick shithouses and thick as fuck.

They were nice(ish) guys, but they could not drink and managed to piss most of us off after a few days. They all chewed tobacco, which they would spit into old beer cans and leave them lying around the mess.

I think they thoroughly hated their stay.

It came to blows when one of them explained he was into wrestling.

Now, let me explain, this is not the 'Big Daddy'/Giant Haystacks British type of wrestling your granny used to get herself off on while watching tele during a Saturday afternoon. Oh, no, this is strange, gay, grappling shite where you wear brightly coloured leotards and roll across the floor while cuddling another man.

A big lad in our mess, a chap called Phill, explained he had done a bit of wrestling a few years back.

The soft Yankee twat challenged him to a match.

Unfortunately for the Yank, Keith's style of wrestling was WWF, no rules Cage fighting, not ivy league.

Keith twatted the poor chap a few times, before holding him down so we could bounce our cocks on his head and rubbed our rusty sheriff's stars in his face.

For some reason, his oppos took offence and some punches started flying.

That's the problem with some 'folks', they don't have a sense of humour.

You may wish to know

Joke

In Jamaica, you can get a steak and kidney pie for £1.75, a chicken and mushroom pie for £1.60 and an apple pie for £2.15.

In St Kitts and Nevis, a steak and kidney pie will cost you £2, a chicken pie (without mushrooms) is £1.70 and a cherry pie can be yours for £1.95.

In Trinidad and Tobago, that steak and kidney pie comes in at £2.50, but you can get two for £3.50, while the chicken and mushroom pie is £2.25, or two for £3.25.
They also offer meat and potato pie for £2, or two for £3. Their apple pies and cherry pies are often sold for £2.75, or any combination of two, for £4.75.

Those are the Pie Rates of the Caribbean.

(Groan!)

Dear John

I was reminded of a Dit I read years ago, in the Gollies Falkland's turnover log.

The dear John went like this:

Dear John,
You have been away from home some 6 months now and in that time, I have been unfaithful to you twice.
I think it would be unfair for you to come home thinking everything was ok when clearly it is not.
Please send me back the photo I sent you.
I hope we will always be friends.
Sadly, and sorry,
Julie.

John, not to be seen off, clears the mess Gronk board of photos and sends them all to Julie, enclosing a note which read as follows,

Dear Julie,
Sorry, luv.
I can't remember which one you are.
Please take your photo from those I enclose and send the rest back.
Ta.
John.

The Scottish Submarine

A Ditty

There was once a sub crewed by Scotsmen,
The redoubtable men of the North.
She patrolled the Atlantic's grey waters
From her base in the Firth of the Forth.

Her Skipper, a dour Aberdonian,
Was known for his tightness with loot,
And much tighter yet with torpedoes,
With a noted reluctance to shoot!

One morning they sighted a tanker
"Let's sink it!" the crew said with glee.
'D'ye know ken the price o' torpedoes?
Forget it, yon tanker's too wee!".

Now while they discussed the expenses,
A destroyer appeared on the scene,
A German, with five-inch artillery,
And she'd spotted the Jock submarine!

They took the boat down in a hurry
While the German came on at a pace.
"Our Skipper'll save us!", the crew said
But the Captain remained Stoney faced!

They sat on the bottom for hours,
Dead quiet, no man made a sound,
While the German let loose her depth charges
And continued to circle around!

Then a voice echoed out in the silence,
In anguish it cried simply this,
"Just fire a bloody torpedo!
Ah'll foot the bill if ye miss!"

Bronington's bump

Ged Dit

Bronington was fitted with Napier Deltics, both for propulsion and the m/s genny (*minesweeping generator*) in 1959.

I joined, just as she was coming out of Rosyth Dockyard hands. There were only two engine room hands aboard, me, as an ME 1 and a Chief Mechanic, Syd.

Syd was a good 'un. We both lived at Cochrane, until the rest of the crew joined.

Anyway, we put to out for sea trials and a fault developed in the starboard gearbox.

The bridge was notified, the CO ordered us to shut down the starboard engine. Dutifully the engine was shut down.
We returned to Rosyth on the Port engine only.

My 'specials' station was the Main Control Room logging manoeuvring movements.

The telegraphs rang for slow ahead starboard, then stop starboard, slow astern starboard and eventually full astern starboard.

The Chief Mech was, during this entire time, trying to get through to the Bridge, to tell them the starboard engine was shut down and we were steaming on the PORT engine only.

Once Syd got through, he was immediately ordered to put the PORT engine full astern.

We did.

The screws started to 'bite', when we hit the dock wall at 7 knots.

It transpired the starboard shaft revolution indicator was wired up to the PORT repeater and vice versa.

As you know (*or not*), the 'Coniston's' had a very high bow, so when the berthing party saw Bronington bearing down on them at great speed and they shat their nicks and legged it.

I did hear later, that the CO leant over the bridge and shouted to the Fo'c'sle Officer to "do something" which he did.... he gave the order "let go both anchors."

We spent six weeks in the floating dock repairing the bows....

Happy days.

Decrepit blue rinse

Gen? Gash? Unsure.

 Few years back on Decrepid ...

After a two-week stopover in Ft Lauderdale for a bit of R&R we bumbled our way over to the Windies,

At some Island, I forget which one, a couple of Cruise Liners tied up alongside.

A few of the lads made a beeline for them, however, as one of the local hotels offered the use of their facilities to the SR mess, it was decided and a couple of us sauntered up for a recce.

The hotel had a swim-up pool bar, loads of sunbeds and looked clean and tidy.

We began to work our way through the cocktail menu.

I picked up a pack of cards, which were left loafing and proceeded to try out the only "card trick" I knew.

The one of three rows of cards, where I can pick the card you guess, well, eventually anywayhow.

I tried it out on some of the American blue rinses who were staying at this hotel. One in particular looked real fit.

Mind you, that was after three rum punches, so even the ugly fat barman was beginning to look half human.

Try as this woman might, she could not work put how the trick was done and bingo, she started to buy the wet's.

I told her, 'don't go away' and disappeared for a piss.

When I returned to the bar the blue rinse gets very amorous with me. So, not wanting to disappoint her, we sauntered to her room for an afternoon 'kip'.

She was heading back to Boston the following morning, so I ended up staying the night. She kept me well watered and entertained until sunrise.

I left early to get back to the ship, promising I would write, which I always meant to do...

Like fuck.

No Die Hard today

W e left Barbados and headed off we were on a drug-busting mission, searching for a cargo vessel called the Northern something or other after receiving intl it was carrying a haul of grade one Columbian chang.

Our chopper spent the best part of two weeks flying around looking for that ship. We eventually found it and two boarding parties, us and the Yanks, began securing it.

We expected the crew to be armed and to offer resistance, so every gun on the upper deck was manned and I had a jimpy on the bridge wing. My young mind had visions of heroics with me blowing up the ship with carefully aimed bursts of fire.

Unfortunately, or fortunately, my Die-Hard moment never came.

No ones did.

Our boarding party searched the ship for days, a team of stokers cut open bulkheads and decks, but we found nothing except for a few small arms.

The ship was kitted out for something as we found hidden storage compartments in the fuel tanks.

But they were all empty, so we had to let the ship go.

We watched as they sailed away into the sunset of the far horizon… or simply steamed off, according to how romantic a spin you want to put on things!

We went to St Lucia to drown our sorrows with dark rum and dusky women.

Just saying...

Jokes

Japanese scientists have created a camera with a shutter speed so fast, they can now photograph a woman with her mouth shut.

A boy asks his granny, 'Have you seen my pills, they were labelled LSD?' Granny replies, fuck the pills, have you seen the dragons in the kitchen.

A woman standing nude in front of a mirror says to her husband: 'I look horrible, I feel fat and ugly, pay me a compliment.' He replies, 'Your eyesight is perfect.'

A mummy covered in chocolate and nuts has been discovered in Egypt ...Archaeologists believe it may be Pharaoh Roche...

Two Indian junkies accidentally snorted curry powder instead of cocaine. Both in hospital...one's in a korma. The other's got a dodgy tikka!

In the first few days of the Olympics, the Romanians took gold, silver, bronze, copper & lead.

Sailing results are in, GB took gold, the USA took silver and Somalia took a middle-aged couple from Weymouth

Wally was a Legend

Gen

Back in 1954, I was on 'Upstart', berthed at Dolphin, waiting to have the boat's bottom scraped.

I got a message that me old oppo, 'Wally' was in Royal Naval Hospital, Haslar.

I took the ferry from the Pompey hard over to Gosport, to go and visit him.

Wally's had his chest, both legs and one arm in plaster.

I asked, "What the hell happened to you?"

Wally said he stole a coppers bike in Gib. So, he could cycle back the docks quickly, so he wasn't adrift.

When he reached the centre gates, he flew down the slope at a great rate of knots, failing to navigate the corner.

The result, he cycled straight into the dry dock.

As he went over the lip, he said he peddled like fuck trying to get to the other side.

He did not make it that far.

The last time I saw Wally, he was in Chatham barracks, on his hands and knees, sweeping the parade ground with a toothbrush.

His tip to me that day was when in deep water, keep your mouth shut.

They don't make legends out of the same stuff nowadays.

This one is true

Gen

Many years ago, I was employed in a local authority

housing department.

My elderly colleague, also an ex-Matelot, collected rents at the front office counter.
Due to his age, he would sometimes lose control of his right arm whilst writing.

He would raise his arm, rarely letting go of his pen, to give himself a rest from writing for a few seconds and wave in the air until he felt comfortable enough to continue.

One day, a lady who was at the desk to pay her rent, asked if waving his arm around ever bothered him.

Without looking up he replied, "Only when I'm standing next to someone in a public toilet, Madam."

Butlins, Barry Island

Gen Dit

I t all started as a bit of fun during a run ashore.

We asked the camp doctor's wife, who was a beautician by trade, to dress and make-up our oppo 'Ricky' as a woman, so we could enter him into the *'Miss Butlins'* weekly beauty competition as a farce to be enjoyed by all.

Not one of us could have guessed how this wind up was to turn out.

Competition day arrived and Ricky, wearing ABBA style metallic hot pants, fishnets, a long-haired blond wig and plentiful makeup appeared on the stage, as a contestant.

The pageant took place, with Ricky playing the part of a girl called 'Wanda Mann'.

No one, it seemed, cottoned on to the fact 'Wanda' was an imposter. Even when 'she' said she wanted to save the world and all the sailors in it.

To cut a long story short, Wanda, AKA Ricky, won the competition.

While the judges were deciding, one of my mates decided to take on some of the holidaymakers at drinking.

He swallowed a whole crate of Guinness and a bottle of whiskey, making him the easy winner.

I guess his Mother would have been proud. Well, until he collapsed in a shitty heap on the deck.

Some other messmates were now entertaining the audience with, 'there once was a lad called Aladdin and the sailor's version of old MacDonalds farm

At this point, no one really cared most of the crowd were so pissed no one cared a jot.

At the bar, Ricky never brought a single drink, because a Spanish waiter, Juan, or Julienne or summit like that, had fallen in love with Wanda and plied her (him) with sticky greens all night.

True Story, but for reasons the names of those involved have been omitted or changed, to protect the (not so) innocent.

Is it me, or was life really that bit simpler in the 'good old days'?

Confession

Gen Dit

I was stationed at HMS CAMBRIDGE in the early part of the 1960s.

During this draft, my mate and I would most often be the last to leave the (NAAFI) bar on a night.

At closing time, the patrol would arrive to make certain the bar was locked and secure.

Just before they came we would fix a large needle to the end of a pool cue, with a strip of harry blackers, and leave it in a 'handy' place.

We would then trot off back to our mess like the caring and well-behaved sailors we were.

However, once the patrol moved on, we would leg-it back to the NAFFI, grab the pool cue with attached spike and poke it through the grill on the shutter of the bar.

The cue was the perfect length to reach packets of Embassy number 6 tipped and Woodbines on the display shelves at the rear of the bar.

There were many rumours and fingers pointed at various individuals regarding the disappearance of the cigarettes.

But my mate and I kept shtumm.... Until now.

Priorities

Joke

My wife came home drunk yesterday.

As she was undressing she stumbled, fell over and passed out.

Knickers round her ankles and pussy on show to the whole world.

Well, what is a man to do?

There was no way I was going to miss a chance like this.

So, I fucked off down the pub with the lads, whilst she slept it off.

'He' told me...

This sound a little whimsical, but I can understand it being told in the mess. I'll rate it as a Gash Dit but I am open to correction.

See what you think.

H e was duty cook during while in a foreign port on a goodwill visit, (*he would not say where or what ship*).

There happened to be a cock and arse party for senior rates.

With most of the ship's company on their runs ashore. 'He' was still turned to, so he could provide the cock & arse buffet in the senior rates mess.

Luckily, it was a cold spread. The other cooks had chipped in with the workload, so all he needed was to get it all onto silvers, take them to the mess and set them on the table.

To make life as easy as possible he decided to set up early and piss off, leaving the collection of the silver flats until the morning.

On his first trip he met a young girl dallying in the senior rates mess. She said she was the daughter of a Chief Greenie and she had flown out to meet the ship earlier that day.

The girl, who remains nameless, followed him back to the galley, offering to help carry some of the food for her father's party. It seems they ended up chatting while he had a fag and swilled down can of CSB on the ships waist.

The pair somehow ended up in the small Catering officer's office, which was located the other side of 2J cross passage, where he shagged her on the victualling officers' desk.

After which the girl helped carry the rest of the spread and finish setting up the buffet, during which time the Chief Greenie/girl's father arrived and she formally introduced them.

As they politely shook hands, he could not help thinking if the Chief could smell his daughter's fanny on his fingers.

Nice end to a duty watch.

Cut it out

Gen

Please note, this is NOT a 'feminine friendly' dit.

Many of you will be familiar with the tedium of deterrent patrol. I found a couple of things which helped ease the mind-blowing monotony.

One was the on-watch wets, the other the 'Chick of the Day'.

For those who do not know about the COTD, a little explanation.

It is primarily the preserve of the SCPOs, whose duty it is to cut out a picture of a 'chick' from one of the many 'maens' magazines such as FHM/Nuts/GQ and so forth.

The 'Chick' then gets pinned on the numbered alarm, corresponding to the day of patrol, for 24 hours.

The SCPOs get judged on the quality of the cutting out, how neat and careful, the removal of any/all distracting background clutter etc. and, of course, the selection of the chosen 'chick' herself.

If this strikes you as male chauvinistic and a bit chavvy, you are absolutely correct. It is.

To this background, add two rather interesting personalities. The first, a barking mad CO with a genuinely unhealthy Gwen Stefani fixation and an MEO from the 1920's, who fell through a wormhole into the future, the future in this case being now.

One of the SCPOs decides to snip an image of Gwen Stefani from one of the aforesaid 'lads mags' and carries out the task with surgical precision.

At this time the old bloke from the 1920's decides to come over all Victorian Puritan and introduces the 'Chick of the Day Standards.'

This meant no more chicks, unless they were clad tastefully, or at least in bikinis which covered all their interesting bits...

Three days after the new 'Chick of the day' standards are introduced, the CO comes for a mess visit. He is proffered the usual wet and as he reaches out his eyes fall upon the Gwen Stefani cut out.

However, because of the new Puritan rules from Mr 1920's, Miss Stefani was now covered by a chunky knit seaman's woolly pully.

The CO asks, "what the fuck is going on with COTD?"

The 1920's MEO pipes up, "I have clamped down on standards of decency sir, in order to maintain..."

"That's a feed of shit MEO and you know it" said a disgruntled Skipper, continuing, "SCPO, cut out a new Chick for today, I want to see some curtains flapping pretty darned quick."

Now, some people take orders a bit too literally.

I started my watch at 03:30 to be confronted by the depths of depravity and perversion, as the new COTD was revealed as a leathery old crow, bent over with rather long, baggy and droopy curtains blowing in the breeze.

Honestly, there are some things even Jack should never see.

Deeps Tartan

Joke

COMMANDER LOGISTICS SUBMARINE FLOTILLA:
TEMPORARY MEMORANDUM 03/16 of 25 Aug 2016

O n behalf of RASM, SubFlot is delighted to announce the availability of a unique tartan, specially woven to represent the Submarine Service, which has been formally registered in the Scottish Register of Tartans as the Official Tartan of the Royal Navy Submarine Service.

The colour scheme has been carefully designed, incorporating black to represent the boats; red, white and blue to represent the RN; green to represent the sea, and gold to represent the coveted submariners' *'Dolphins'* badge.

Produced by the House of Edgar, this premium quality tartan, as well as a bespoke kilt and trews, service for optional wear as part of No. 2 uniform, is now available to all submariners. The material is also available by the metre... BLAH BLAH...

...the Submarine tartan represents one of several projects designed to enhance both the esprit-de-corps and corporate identity of the Submarine Service.

The material offers a unique opportunity for submariners to differentiate themselves from other members of the Armed Forces and it is hoped that the tartan will become synonymous with the elite force that is the Royal Navy Submarine Service...

"Almost dropping his Litre of Buckie, Hamish mumbles incoherently whilst shuffling off into the gloaming".

Then, overheard in the 'Burgh:

Skimmer, "See you, Jimmy, whits yon kiltie youse be awerring?"
Deeps, "Tis newly-wefted for The Trade Clan"

Skimmer, Jings! Nivver hurd o' thet ilk - Gizza cloo will ye, hoose the Chieftie o' yon Clan?"

Deeps, "Don'tcha know? I guess that would be 'Our Wullie' to you, pal".

Skimmer, (*Aghast*) "You dinnae mean......Himselfie?"

Deeps, "Aye, 'tis Prince William, Duke of Cambridge, KG, KT, PC, ADC(P) Commodore-in-Chief of the Royal Navy Submarine Service".

Skimmer, "So help ma' Boab"

Dirty posh totty

Gash?

In my younger days, copping off was never a problem.

One of the most memorable was a young lady, let's call her Penny. (*Although, Penelope was her real name.*)

Penny was a gorgeous curvaceous brunette with many great assets.

She spoke well, Swiss finishing school well, all very jolly hockey sticks and such like, oh, she also had a filthy mind and unquenchable thirst for rampant sex.

At the time she was a studying art and was slumming it as a penniless student in a shared house. Although Penny was far from penniless, as was attested with her car, a spanking new Mercedes which Daddy bought as a nineteenth birthday gift.

As it happens, Penny's room was on the ground floor of the house, which was fantastic for me as she loved leaving the window open, primarily so I could clamber in and play the part of a perverted, sex deprived, burglar or such like.

You see, she liked a bit of a tousle and some disgusting, degrading stuff whispered into her ears as she was taken advantage of.

It was a fetish with her.

The more depraved and sicker the things whispered into her ears the more she squirmed and begged to be 'used'.

I was willing to play my part to keep her happy and satisfied.

This one night she was at some 'girls' party, make-up, cooking pots, clothes, sex toys, who knows? But it was a 'ladies only' affair.

She asked if I would climb through the window and 'take her' straight away, no foreplay, no sweet talk, just slip in and 'help myself'. *(Her words, not mine.)*

Of course, I could not let Penny down, after all I was a gentleman and had made a promise.

I think it was around two-thirty, that's 02:30 Hrs in real time.

I pulled the duvet from the bed and leapt onto her. She was face down and still snoring.

I knew she would soon wake when I started pounding away so, following orders I plunged on in there.

Suddenly a figure arose next to me and said, "wrong girl," before beginning to laugh her head off.

I looked at Penny as I stopped thrusting into myself... into the other girl who was totally comatose...

Penny found the whole thing utterly amusing and said her sister was staying after being far to pissed to go home and it was her I had accidentally slid into.

The Admiral

One from a Booty, Gen

Whilst I was a young skin on Fearless, we docked at Sevastapol.
Awesome run ashore, beer, wine, vodka, all at stupidly low prices.
Three whores cost a fiver. What fun that was... (*I am told*).

The Russian empire was crumbling.

The cold war over and the Ruskies had not got to grip with capitalism yet.

The downside; as we were the first British warship to visit Sevastopol the ship was full of Top Brass. Scrambled egg and some 'other' important people.

We were only allowed 'Cinderella' runs ashore, Jack wearing number ones and Lovats for us Booties.

All went well for the first few hours. Predictably, things got out of hand as the night wore on.

With all the 'top brass hanging around there was a constant stream of high ranking officers getting piped on and off the ship.

The gangplank sentries and the OOW were getting run ragged and sore lipped.

Now, about 01:00 ish, this night/morning I was on gangway duty when we saw this Russian Admiral sauntering towards the ship.

There was no mistaking the uniform, big hat, chest full of medals and all. So, as we were instructed we called out the watch to give the boarding dignitary the full naval protocol his rank demanded.

Hurriedly, the watch formed a guard of honour just in time to welcome the Admiral aboard with the correct pipe.

The Admiral struggled a bit with the steep incline as he climbed up the gangplank with the plank, one step forward two backwards. Eventually making it to the deck where he was met with a formal salute.

He thanked the lads for turning out in a clear and recognisable Scouse accent, saying there really was no need to make such a fuss.

Scouse said he brought the uniform in some bar earlier for the bargain price of ten quid!

End of the Watch

(Gen)

It was one of those busy watches, the ones that are non-stop.

Until it went deadly quiet just before the end of watch. So, we all relaxed and began chatted away, passing the last few moments of duty by keeping one eye on the clock.

One of the phones ring and 'Trisha', our 'new' baby Jenny answered.

"Comcen, how can I help you?"

Nothing else was happening, so we all tuned in, watching Trisha and waiting to find out what the call was about.

Trisha's jaw dropped, and she visibly turned an ashen colour.

Covering the 'phones mouthpiece with her hand she spoke to the Leading Wren.

"This guy says he's going to kill himself, what do I say?" she asked.

"Pass me the phone, Trisha", said the Leading Wren beckoning with her hand, "I'll sort it out".

The Leading Wren listened took the 'phone and pressed it to her ear.

We were all silent. I think everyone was holding their breath.

After a few seconds of intense listening, the Leading Wren spoke.

"Well, that depends, BIG BOY. Do you like leather or I would you like me to bring a couple of friends and we could all have a gang bang? Now, PISS OFF you stupid fucking Bastard", she screamed the last few words into the mouthpiece and slammed the phone down.

Turning to Trisha, she asked, "what on earth made you think he was going to kill himself?"

Trisha, obviously an innocent Jenny, said,

"He said he was going to toss himself off. I thought he meant he was going to jump off a building, or a bridge, or something."

The entire Comcen erupted in a raucous howl of laughter.

Poor little Trisha.

I guess she soon learned the meaning of life though.

Kerplunk and ganga

T his time I had drawn the Morning/Afternoon watch (*1am until 7am - 1pm until 7pm*) which I loathed because you eat lunch for your breakfast when you get up for your afternoon watch.

After stopping every small boat in the area which had room to hide a single spliv, so that was all of them, we stopped a boat with a middle-aged Aussie couple onboard. They were supplementing their pensions by doing a coke run.

We recovered around sixty million quid's worth, not including the stuff they threw overboard before we got close enough to stop them.

I think it was one of the largest seizures at the time.

After that, we popped into Puerto Rico. The American naval base of Roosevelt Roads. The base is larger than the town, Ceiba, where it is based.

Anywayhow, on leaving the Naval base and heading towards Ceiba (turn right), we came across a small bar called El Coqui, which was run by a very accommodating lady.

Once you managed to 'kiss the butterfly' on her bars ceiling,

Without using your hands, you were made a very welcome guest.

In fact, we never ventured any further that night and, in the early hours, were driven back to the base in her rather large and loud American car. I think it was called a Mach1 and had something to do with a pony and some chap named Shelby.

A shortstop in The Azores for a bit of bronze-ying before heading home to Pompey. It was in the Azores the lads getting first leave tried to wind us up by scribbling 'FLIB' (*First Leave Is Best*) all over the ship before fucking off for their flights home.

The night before we docked at Pompey we anchored off Southsea. That is worse than spending a wasted night in Falmouth harbour.

If you listened carefully you could hear the ten to two's leaving Joanna's salubrious establishment

It didn't stop us celebrating though.
It was like an extra Channel night, we got totally wasted. Even the old man came down to the mess for a quick CSB.

We stuck one of the new skins to the deckhead with Harry Blackers and played a sort of human kerplunk, taking turns to tear a strip off until the poor unfortunate kid fell onto the deck.

The kiddo got a beer, the winner got to be stuck on the roof, so we could play again.

I am damned sure my nose is bent to the left from me hitting the deck the night.

Great days indeedy.

Only idiots prat with the Marines

Pete is sitting in the QMs lobby at Neptune's internal gate, sipping his stand easy coffee while ruminating on how good life is.

Just three weeks left before his retires to civvy street is reached. Up until then it's QM duties, 3 weeks on 2 weeks off, not a bad routine to finish with.

Looking up from his coffee he watches as a Pussers Tilly parks where it should not stop. A Leading Regulator climbs out.

"Strange," thinks the QM Pete, the said Crusher is not wearing any webbing.

The Crusher marches into Pete's polished lobby and plants himself in front of the full-length mirror pulling, tugging and brushing his blue suit.

Pete thinks to himself, "it's the Commanders Table this morning and this man must be in for an award."

"Good Morning, Leading Reg," says QM Pete, always willing to show a happy face. "Are you going up for your third badge this morning?"

"No, I fucking aren't," screamed the Crusher, "get off that fucking chair and start acting in a seamanlikc manncr, you greasy submariner you."

"Nice!" thought Pete, but about par for the course.

"Report to the reg office after your watch. Tell them I said you must have a regular service haircut." bawled the Crusher twat before marching off towards the Admin block.

As it happens, next to the QMs Lobby, was the office of the OCRM, which he shared with his Sergeant Major, a Colour Sergeant of the RM Provost Branch.

Both gentlemen were ensconced in the said office, munching on the tasty eggy bacon butties and drinking hot coffee, made by Pete five minutes before the knob-head Crusher arrived.

"Was that man who just left your lobby the same prick who jumped out of that illegally parked Tilly?" asked the OCRM.

"Yes sir," says Pete, "the very same person."

"Did I hear him swear, Pete?"

"Yes Sir," indeed you did, sir," replied Pete honestly.

"Was he swearing at you, QM?"

"I'm afraid so sir."

"Did he slam the door, making a loud bang and upsetting my stand easy?"

"Oh, yes Sir, and he used the Booties mirror to preen himself in."

"Utterly disgraceful," muttered the Officer.

"May I make a suggestion, Sir?" pipes up Coulors.

"It seems some of our Royal Marines are a bit rusty on vehicle search procedures. Perhaps I should have some of them hone their skill in this highly technical operation, much as practised in Northern Ireland?"

"What a splendid idea Sergeant Major; carry on," adding, "remember to ensure all seats are removed, as per SOP's and checked, especially those in that Pussers Tilly's which is illegally parked."

The SM set about mustering his band of Booties.

After a short while, the OCRM shouted for Pete.

"Have you ever watched a thorough vehicle search?"

"No Sir," Pol replied.

"Come and watch this then," said OCRM "you may learn something."

The Booties were professionals. Within a few minutes the Crushers Tilly was divided into its various components; seats out, engine mangled, spare wheel stripped, linings ripped, dashboard on the pavement, wires hanging out of every electrical orifice.

It was a wonderful sight to behold.

Eventually, the Booties wandered off for some scran, leaving the dismembered vehicle scattered over the tarmac.

Pete had a very short 'service' standard haircut during his lunch.

Later that day the OCRM said, "Nice haircut Pete! By the way, I have news of that Crusher who parked in the wrong place."

"Do you, Sir" Pete replied.

"Indeed, I do. The Jaunty trooped him for scraping the paintwork on the Patrol Tilly. He got a hefty fine I hear."

Moral of the story:

Only idiots Fuck with the Marines. That's Sub or Royals!

Always first in the Queue

(Gen?)

Joining the Cherry B at Rosyth in 1973 and immediately sailed to Iceland for a 6-week patrol. (This was during the 'Cod War').

I was given DHP duties and I a quick learner, the quicker you cleaned up after scran, the quicker you could climb into your pit for some big zeds.

The Killick Reg was a total twat.

He made sure he was first in the queue for every afternoon for watchman's scran, even though he didn't keep watches.

Usually, the North Sea was as rough as fuck. Most of the time it was difficult to stay sat down, never mind eat your scran, the smell in the scullery was bogging and I spent a lot of time with my head in the big steel sink calling for Huey.

On one particularly the Gophers were huge, giving us a right pounding.

I set up the dining hall for lunch, put out the cutlery and condiments. On the edge of the counter, I placed a fanny of gravy, custard and soup just as normal

I open the dining hall hatch and, as usual, in marched the LREG in half blues.

Right at that moment the ship made a large roll to Starboard and because neither Buster Brown or I had put out the non-slip mats, one if the steel fannys slid off the counter, the lid flying off followed by thick brown sludge the cook called gravy, which, as it happens, decided to land on the LREGs nice clean, ironed and starched, white front.

Now, to say no one laughed until they split a gut would be a little bit of a porkie pie.

I think he spent for day sick, smothered in some paste or cream the doc gave him.

For those four days, the ship ran more smoothly and happily than ever.

Oh, and for some reason, the word 'retribution' kept springing to mind.

Not Pusser

This one's from Pongo, but I have allowed into Jack's Dits because we have all been there.

Read on, you'll soon see what I mean.

We've all been there.

You know, that situation where you have been made to look a total and utter twat by one of your seniors/DS.

I am certain each person who has been in this situation has, in their dreams, planned revenge.

As Junior Leaders, we got our fair share of shite and beats (*no children's act as such in '89*) from our DS, as we were the 'leaders of the future'.

On one field exercise (*we spent virtually all our time in the field, hence the nickname "Cabbages"*) I fell foul of an evil Sergeant, who for OPSEC reasons will be known as Smith.

Now Smith did not like me and called me a "Cocky London bastard", all because of one simple little incident, which I shall now reveal...

Imagine the scene, it is bloody freezing cold, we are on one of the Catterick training areas and young JL Cpl Blackrat is making a nice hot brew with his last packet of coffee.

Smith says to me, "Making a brew are you sonny?"

I nodded and said "yes".

He states, "I can't find my mug", hinting he wanted my brew.

I was against giving him a swig of my hot brew. I thought him a crabby bastard, unclean teeth, halitosis and such. I am sure his breath could revive a corpse.

However, if I refused it would have been like signing my death warrant, so I politely I said, "Would you like a bit Sgt?"

"Do bears shit in the woods?"

Quick as flash I quipped, "Not in these woods, they don't"

Smith snarled, decked me with a straight right jab and walked off with my brew. Ten minutes later, he threw my mug back and, as it bounced off my head, I silently swore I would kill the fucker.

That evening, I volunteered to do stag at 0200hrs. I had already planned my revenge.

Being on compo for three days, I had not yet had a good shit, but I knew I would not need to wait long from the way my guts were rumbling and my farts stank.

At 0200hrs, I took up position in the forward trench and waited for about the minutes.

I knew Smith's basha was at the other end of the Platoon harbour area. As stealthy as a Gurkha who needs one more ear to complete his necklace, I moved silently towards the swine's basha.

Outside of his route in, I took off my webbing, laid my weapon upon it, dropped my combats and kecks and proceeded to curl out a turd the size of a large python, right beside his head.

Now, this is not as easy as it sounds.

When you have a compo crap, your ring stretches to the dimensions of the large hadron collider to let loose the beast that lay within.

(*It does not help if you are giggling inanely to yourself either*).

Anyway, Job done, I placed my used squares of shithouse paper neatly, and deeply, into the toecaps of said Sgt Smith's boots.

Back at my stag position, I waited for the inevitable fall out.

A few hours later during stand to, I heard an almighty scream from the far end harbour area. It sounded like someone screaming "Which one of you dirty fuckers has put shit roll in my boots? Someone is going to die".

This was nothing in comparison to the noise he made when exiting his basha.

"Arrrrrggghhh, I've put my hand in a massive shit. I'm going to find you, you fucking fucker, I will kick the fuck out of your fucking head, you fucking fucker."

Everyone found it bloody hilarious, even the other DS's.

I was still laughing when the twat tabbed us for ten miles in full kit.

From Russia with Love

Gen

F169-Amazon.

Whilst 'skimming' about in the Irish Sea, playing war games and escorting a convey of cross-channel ferries.

We had to protect the same from a dastardly sludgemarine which was lurking somewhere *'out there'*.

Not wishing to make you deeps types feel too good about yourselves, but we never did get a contact, many *'green grenades'* were sighted shooting up from the 'oggin, but we never got on top of that sludgemarine (*Nuclear – attack?*).

At the end of the exercise, I was closed up in the Ops Room, when the sonar chaps shouted they had a contact.

Coming up from the rear, at warp factor lots. It was that elusive sludgemarine itself, which proceeded to overtake, underneath us, playing *'From Russia with love'* on the underwater telephone.

Very apt.

It did make us laugh, even though we were vanquished skimmers.

More Murphy's Laws

6. Those who live by the sword, get shot by those who don't.

7. Nothing is foolproof to a sufficiently talented fool.

8. The 50-50-90 rule: Anytime you have a 50-50 chance of getting something right, there's a 90% probability you'll get it wrong.

9. It is said that if you line up all the cars in the world end-to-end, someone from California would be stupid enough to try to pass them.

10. If the shoe fits, get another one just like it.

Could you Imagine?

A Gen, Deeps tale.

It has nothing to do with John Lennon.

Could you imagine if one of the cooks started the Hobart spud peeler, not having told or got permission to do so from the control room.

Then, can you imagine me in the sound room at the same moment, as controller, reporting a high bearing rate contact very close on the starboard side on Passive and marking Searcher grade three moving aft.

After which could you possibly imagine all the back aft Tiffs in the SR's mess having a good laugh, because the deck ape in the sound room classified the spud peeler as a submarine and sending the boat to CQS.

Imagine me in the SR's mess afterwards, proving to these clankies that OSN does not have a bearing rate change, that the contact was in fact an lmv convergence zone detection (*we were doing warp factor six at the time and had a new bow dome that reduced flow noise to zero - even at 28kts*), and telling the clankies, I never once mentioned the word submarine in my contact report.

Imagine me, all five feet six of (*now*) pure bile and throat ripping, spitting, snarling deck ape telling a six-two NCOW to wind his fucking neck in, until he knows just what the hell he's talking about and recommending he comes up to the sound room and does a watch or two, just like WE had to do when qualifying systems back aft.

Imagine a NCOW ho, ho, ho-ing and trying to make light of the fact he got a bite.

BITE... fucking BITE... have I ever gone back aft and called his professionalism into question over anything to do with engines... EVER.

Then, a nice friendly hand on the shoulder from the Coxswain with the words...

"Ignore him, the man's a twat and he won't be with us much longer. He's going inboard... he's done his six months at sea".

It still annoys me, even now, 175 million years later.

If I saw him in a pub now I'd buy him a beer, put Senokot granules in it and then ho, ho, ho, as he shits himself.

Then I would chortle and say, "What's wrong twat, can't you take a bite".

... Just saying...

One from a Crabfat

But worth sharing, because it is so horribly fascinating, it must be a Gen Dit.

I walked into the block washrooms in Germany one Sunday morning to find, ramrod straight, with no kinks, a huge turd balancing between the hot and cold water taps on the boot cleaning sink.

The distance between said taps was approximately 30cms.
I still wonder to this day how this was done.

Did the offender squat over the taps to commit the deed? (*Clearly moving forward to drape said steamer on said taps*).

Did he shite on some cardboard and drape the poo over them?

Was it removed from the karzi and manipulated onto the plinth using his oppo's racing spoons?

It was such an amazing sight, it was still there three days later.

It was a Turner prize winner without a doubt.

Even the Flight Sergeant came along, had a shufti and stated, that impressive as this specimen was, he saw a chum of his lay a cable the size of a reticulated Python in Belize, and then watched on as a pig came along and scoffed it.

This beast, however, was untouched by man or pig.

I still have no idea how it came to be, or where it went.
Nuff said.

Jimmy & the Flight deck Scupper

Gen

My last deployment was aboard Gurkha, 1979. (As WIGS).

I was in charge of a working party tasked with clearing a scupper which drained the flight deck.

The port side of the flight deck was putrid, a fouls stink which made us baulk. There was a mingin puddle of slime developing which made me heave just looking at it.

Anyway, I traced the blockage to a scuppers outlet a couple of metres above the waterline, port side, below the hangar.

My best stoker went over the side on a bosuns chair with a charged kinetic gun. He was ready to blow back the choked scupper as soon as he received my orders.

Back on the flight deck I checked all was clear due to the inevitable 'blow back' that the kinetic gun would produce, only to find the Jimmy and half the wardroom up there using it as a temporary meeting room.

The Jimmy, who was a little fat turd, was strutting his stuff and gobbing off like a superhero.

I stood at a respectful distance, patiently waited for him to pause for a breath.

When he did stop spouting for a millisecond, I saluted and gave an explanation of why I wanted the space.

The Jimmy said, "Fuck off. NOW, Leading Hand and do your fucking job. Do NOT fucking interrupt me again".

The rule is, always obey the last order, right? So, I said, "Yes Sir" and made my way down to the ships waist, leaned over the side so my best Stocker could see me clearly and gave him the go ahead to blast the scupper.

BLURRURPPPFFHH, off went the kinetic gun with full force into the scupper, forcing the blockage and all the shite collected above out, clearing the pipework as planned.

Almost instantly I heard howls of indignation and sounds of gipping and borking from the flight deck above. Just as I informed the Jimmy, all the slimy, shitty, stinking water and gunk covered the assembled wardroom members including the Jimmy himself.

On the waist I was pissing my bollock off.

The Jimmy wanted my guts for that little incident but could do nothing about it, as it was he who issued the order.

Oh, happy times indeed.

A Gen, Gash Dit

My oppo always volunteered to ditch the gash from the MCO during the morning watch.

He said it was because he enjoyed watching the sunrise.

Truth is, he enjoyed an early morning cuppa and a morning spliv with his oppo, the ships cook.

Happy Daze.

Malta, Donkeys & the Britannia Bar

So, off we go ashore in Malta and head straight for the Gut.

Its Sunday and we were about to ascend into the pit, when our attention is drawn to activity in the form of loads of bodies going into the bar.

On the right-hand side of the hill as you entered the Gut, is the "Britannia bar".

You entered by going downstairs and into a massive room with a bar along each end. Around the bar there was an upstairs mezzanine floor and the place was reminiscent of an old swimming pool without the pool.

Anyway, we shuffle up to the bar and grab the last two stools and set to drinking.

Next to us is a canteen manager off another canoe, his civvy oppo and the chief airy fairy off our ship.

It was at this time of my life I had taken a keen interest in making music. The like of my music had never been heard before, except when the odd dockyard Feral was run over. I had bought a harmonica in Honky Fid and fancied I could play it. (I can now, but then...) Trouble is, I was not deterred by the abundant threats to put me ashore even when at sea.

I set to playing; low and behold, I manage a reasonable rendering of Jimmy crack corn. The Sceptics are all loving it and are all clapping, stomping feet and singing.

The chief wafoo is not loving it and offers to stow my mouth organ in my shit locker. I decline his offer by politely telling him to go fuck himself, at which point the can man smacks me in the phizog.
Immediately, think this is very impolite, and reciprocate with a left hook.

The chief wafoo seems to think I require another dig and proceeds to deliver it. At this point, wally does a Superman impersonation and leaps several feet in the air, launches a kick in the chest at the can man, but hits the chief. The can mans' oppo jumps up and at that point everyone is belting each other. The chief goes down, the can man's oppo does as well, and the can man legs it.

The bouncers pin me down, and Wally soon gets the same treatment.

Then Wally breaks free and hits the biggest Yankee sailor this side of Nagasaki. War breaks out. The doormen are fighting the yanks to stop them killing me and Wally.

Order is restored and the doormen tell us their plan. We get to walk out, they lock the doors and keep the yanks in for 5 minutes. We escape and then they liberate the sceptics.

So out we go. Trouble is Wally tells me he ain't running from yanks.

I tell him let's pretend their Russians and can we FRO. "No, we can't," comes the expected answer, we fight or die.

It's the "die" bit that gets my attention, as I have had near death experiences before with Wally, many the time I nearly got killed ashore with him.

So, we stay. Outcome the sceptics 7 in number, but we have a master plan.

Ambush.

We strike as they emerge and there are quickly only 4 standing.

Yeah, four fuckin great hairy Neanderthals who set about trying to make me ugly and bleed. Wally has another plan, ... run.... and off he goes.
We run, and run, and run straight into the shore patrol from St Angelo.

They want to have a chat and ask why we are running away from the seventh cavalry. Wally implements plan C, this involves decking the leading patrolman. Then he runs, ... I follow and the yanks, who have now arrived, start fighting with the patrol. We escape into an ally with a low wall which we easily jump, straight into, ...Shite.

Gallons and gallons of it, and did I mention that for whatever reason *(some service event or other)* we are wearing ...6's and for the uninformed, that's a white sailor suit.

When I say white I mean that's the colour Pusser intended it to be when he gave it to me. Mine is now a lot like the multicoloured dream coat except there is no white present.

I am sitting in a stable full of Maltese donkeys who are shitting like it's going out of fashion and mostly on me. One was kind enough to try and get some off me by simply p1ssing over me.

Wally now to cheer me up points out the plus side to our situation, we have shaken off the patrol and the Yanks.

This cheers me up no end.

All we must do now is try not to attract attention, and bumble back to Selina creek and go aboard, and the jobs a good un.

Going down the Pub

Joke

After a short but passionate courtship Jack married Jenny.

Two weeks after they returned from honeymoon, Jack fancied a night out with the lads. A good sesh out on the town, a bit of a party with his old Oppo's.

So, he said to his new wife, Jenny, "Honey, I'll only be a few hours" and started for the door.

"Where are you going, Coochy Coo?" asked Jenny.

"I'm going to the pub, my pretty faced little darling. I'm going to have a beer."

Jenny said, "You want a beer, my love?"

She opened the door to the fridge and there were 20 different kinds of beer and lager, brands from 12 different countries: Singapore, India, Australia, America, Brazil, as well as South and North England.

Jack did not know what to say. He was amazed his new wife was so sensitive to his needs, but he really wanted a night out, without upsetting her.

The only thing he could think of saying was, "Thank you my little Lollipop...but at the pub they have special glasses for each beer, it makes it taste better and... "

Jack never got to finish his sentence, because Jenny held a finger to his lips and said, "You want a special glass, my lover?"

She pulled a huge box of glasses from under the sideboard, there was a 'special' glass for every lager and beer in the fridge.

Jack turned pale, wondering how he would get out of this one. "Yes, Tootsie roll, but at the pub they have snacks, they are really delicious...I won't be too long. I promise".

Jack had only taken one more step towards the front door when Jenny replied. "You want snacks, Poochie?"

She opened the larder. It was piled high with a whole range of crisp snacks, pork scratching, nuts and cheesy bites.

In the lower part of the fridge were pigs in blankets, buffalo wings, jalapeno poppers, pork pies and onion bhajis.

"Oh, thank you my sweetest honey," Jack said, thinking as fast as he could, "but at the pub there's man talk, swearing, dirty words and all that stuff".

Jack put a hand on the latch, freedom was now only a single footstep away.

"You want dirty words, Cutie Pie?
...Listen up dickhead. Sit down, shut the fuck up, drink your damn beer, from your damn special glass. Eat your fucking snacks. Because you are now married and you are not going to a fuckin' pub! That shit is over... Now, you got that through your thick skull, you twat?"

It is said, by Jenny, they lived happily ever after from that day on.

Jack was not available for comment.

Oh, South Carolina

Gen Dit from, Charleston Naval Shipyard, South Carolina, US of A.
In the year Nineteen Hundred and God Knows what.

HMS Courageous tied up alongside.

Morning, approximately 07.55am.

The trot sentry piped "5 minutes to colours, ratings detailed, close up..."

Through the accommodation space hatch, they come.
One goes front-wards towards the Jack Staff, the other slides around the fin, heading back aft.

Milliseconds later he is back and is greeted by the OOD.

"If you want to pull the Ensign up fill yer pigging boots, 'cos I 'aint fucking going back there, mate", he says to the Officer of the Day.

The OOD, being somewhat peeved at his subordinate refusing to do his duty, commenced a shit fit, promising the rating stoppage of leave/subbies/gratuitous sex with Yank grippos and to endure all manner of punishment and evil torture, if he does not get the flag up sharpish.

The rating thrusts Ensign into OOD's hands and tells him to, "Do colours your fucking self".

OOD - now dazed and confused proceeds around the outboard fin, but halfway he and makes instant U-turn and re-joins the colour party, who are still gathered by accommodation space hatch.

The reason for all this was that draped around the Ensign Staff was the biggest fuck off alligator/crocodile-thingy-beasty- monster ever seen by anyone on the ship.

The fact it was the only one any of them had ever seen is beside the point.

That day we used the bridge flagpole for colours and called the Yank Plod in to deal with the nasty looking reptilian behemoth.

Footnote: *Nobody went aft to read the draft marks at night after that, they did it from the jetty instead.*

One from a Jenny

A Gen excerpt from my Naval interview...

Male PO: "We see your old man was a Marine. What does he think of you joining up?"

Me, (*cocky-know-it-all-teen*), "He's not so happy, because he thinks all Wrens are groundsheets for Sailors".

Cue both Senior Rates looking at each other, stifling smirks of laughter.

Male PO: (*barely managing to keep it together*) "And what do you think about that statement?"

Me: (*proud and confident*) "I don't really understand what it means, but I'm sure I'll find out for myself".

Exit, one happy naive teen, thinking she aced it.

Raucous laughter echoing throughout the recruiting office.

At home, when I relayed the conversation, one very embarrassed and not so happy ex-Booty Dad.

Ps. I got the job!

Shite for Brains

Gen

Raleigh in 1987.

I was a 17-year-old Tiff apprentice in basic training.

I lost my ID card during PT and was issued with a temp card.

However, once got back in our block, my mate Taffy found my ID card. Somehow, perhaps because they were newly laminated, it became stuck to the bottom of his own card.

I Thought this was great news and went back to discipline office to tell them I found my original ID card.

The WOMAA (WRNS) asked me to return the temporary card issued a short while ago.

The conversation was along these lines:

Me *"I ripped it up."*

WOMAA *"You ripped it up. What?"*

At this point any Common Dog I had fell out of my arse

Me *"I ripped it up, Chief."*

Her *"Do I look like a chief?"*

Me *(panicking)* *"Sorry MASTER."*

I could see a couple of Reggies stifling laughter, however worse was to follow.

The WOMAA (WRNS) has now turned a bright shade of scarlet and is about to blow a gasket.

I did not have a single thought of what to call her, so my shite for brains gave me a genius suggestion, *"errrrrr MISTRESS,"* I blurted out.

A scary moment of silence followed, only pierced by the sound of the Reggies bursting out with raucous laughter when they could no longer hold in their mirth.

That was the point I decided to leave my dignity behind and legged it, in fear for my life.

Dues where they're due though, I never heard anything about that incident afterwards. Perhaps the entertainment I provided was payment enough?

Although, during some of my more restless nights I can still hear the laughter echoing from the office as the door swings shut behind me.

Sponsored Row

Gen Dit from a sundodger

We were doing a sponsored row, you know the sortof thing, some place gives the ship an exercise bike, a treadmill or a rowing machine and everyone has a go to try and raise a few bob for some charity or other.

Our task was to row the same distance as it is from Faslane to New York.

One of the writers in the Josses office calculated that, at a steady 32 rpm, with each of the ship's company taking turns, we could row for 30 mins each and complete the said task in the time allocated.

We were on patrol, so the challenge was a novelty which helped pass the time.

Anyway, this day the sound room picked up a threat tonal, it seemed to be a Victor 3.

(It was nothing to bother us, so we cracked on with the rowing).

The Skipper initially showed a bit of interest, but it tied in with the int report, so was not too worried.

We then lost the contact in some "Bio".

The charity row was going well, we all made it part of our daily routine.
Besides, it was a good way to make a bit of money for a kid's hospice up near Loch Lomond somewhere.

During the morning watch, the Victor 3 turned up again.

Skipper was called. We cleared stern arcs a few times, but he was still there. Sound room was totally confused as they could not get a bearing, the Victor 3 was on 2007 and not on towed array.
Skipper called the boat to action stations and the contact disappeared.

We stood down after a few hours.

Soon we were back to normal routine and carried on rowing and guess what, Victor 3 turned up again.

Sound room and the CHOPS(S) did not have a clue until a TAS rating piped up, "I know what it is," he said.

You have guessed, a Victor 3 has the same tonals as a standard rowing machine.

We lost the first (and still carried on with rowing,) as the rowing was blanked out by "bio" and "shore noise" or so our sound room said.

So, on a multibillion-pound Polaris submarine, even the simplest thing, like a sponsored row can cause havoc.

I would like to add a disclaimer to any technical buffs out there if my technical info is incorrect, it is due to me leaving the submarine service over 12 years ago.

But it did happen cos, I was there.

Knob-Head and the Encrypted Signal

Many years ago...

I was a young fresh-faced junior flag-wagger in Her Majesty's Reserve Navy. Whenever the opportunity arose, it was off to sea for the weekend.

I was on duty in the comms dept this particular weekend, along with two trained comms staff. I was on the tactical comms ccts on the bridge and my oppo was in the wireless office below.

We also happened to have a complete, new out of the box, novice with us.

On Saturday, we received an encrypted signal.

Running to the crypto safe, my colleague duly retrieved all relevant publications and proceeded to decrypt it.

After half an hour, he calls for assistance, so the new boy and I begin to help, but with no success.

... It turns out the signal was incorrectly encrypted, but that is not the dit...
Being unable to offer any more help, I leave him alone and head to the bridge for some fresh air.

The 'oggin then decided to get a bit busy and soon the sea-state was around eight or nine.

My colleague, not one for anything rougher than the ripples in a cup of tea, decided it was time to talk on the big white telephone and legs it to the heads, leaving thc trainee, (*let's call him Knob-Head*), to keep an eye on the office.

We return to shore the next day and conduct the hand-over with the permanent staff in the usual manner:

"Everything OK?"
"Yes"
"Anything missing?"
"No"
"Fine, pass me that chit and I'll sign for it all"

Next day at work, I get a phone call from a Chief who seems to be in a bit of a panic. He asked me about the crypto; I reported I'd left the office before the decryption was completed.

He then asked if I shredded anything, anything at all, especially any short bits of tape which may have been a different colour from the normal backroll tape.

It turns out, while my colleague was puking up his ring in the heads, Knob-Head took it upon himself to do some tidying up. He shredded all the odd bits of paper from the failed decryption attempts, that is all the TP backroll and paper tape, including the current crypto segment.

The Chief who was calling me went through all the shreddy bags from that weekend and (*happily*), managed to convince his boss there were enough shreddings of the appropriate colour that the 'missing' segment was also, be it inadvertently, shredded and...

"if you will just sign here to witness its destruction, boss, you'll never have to buy another beer again."

Unsure about the last bit though!

Lotus Blossom's Revenge

Thailand

C rashed out on the sofa, watching a film set in Thailand where some scenes showed matelots pissing up and merrymaking in the bars.

It brought back a memory...

We were in Bangkok. Half a dozen of us on a run ashore when we found ourselves in a bar where the 'Ladies' danced for whatever they could collect.

Now, in those days, money was actually worth something, so a pocket full of coins would go a long way. *(The smallest note was Ten Bob, that's equivalent to fifty pence nowadays, but then Ten Bob was a month's pay for Jack.)*

As was the done thing, I placed a baht coin on the top of one of the bottles strategically sited around the edge of the stages in the bar.

Along comes Lotus Blossom, or whatever she was called, who was bollocky buff of course, lowers herself down over the bottle and picks up the coin with her flaps.

Lotus Blossom smiles in appreciation, as she drops the coin in her tips tin, before thrusting her gash at me, allow me a quick fondle or to kiss it, as is customary.

Following the advice of a three badge Stoker, I repeated this action several times. Each time she does her routine letting us lads have a slightly longer play each time.

Once convinced she is onto a good thing, we go in for the kill.

Out of her sight, we Hold the next coin between two dead matchsticks, so not to burn our fingers as we heat it with the flame from a zippo.

One the coin was just slightly less hot than the surface of the Sun, we place it on the bottle top as we had done with the previous coins.

Lotus Blossom sidles over, swaying her hips and pelvic thrusting, squats and collects the coin with her flaps as expected... but you could tell by her expression she was not amused, not one fucking bit.

After a minute or two she resumes dancing.

Now, the Three Badger told me one more thing, which I 'forgot' to share with the other lads. So, I am on high alert for what I the Stoker told me would happen next.

And happen it did, just as he said.

Lotus Blossom smiled at us and slowly dances towards us, twirling swirling and gyrating each and every which way. She was putting on a far more intense show than before.

Some of the lads were still laughing and jeering about the hot coins, that is until Lotus Blossom, right on the edge of the stage, turned her back to us and bends forward, exposing it all.

At this point I leg it to the far end of the bar-room, escaping just in time as Lotus Blossom pisses over most of the lads by waving her pissy pussy side to side as she lets spray.

One of the lads tries shoving a beer bottle up her shitty brown sheriff's star, but by then the heavies are closing in and we all get slung out onto the street.

Three bars down, with most of the lads smelling of whore's piss, we find a bar with dancing girls and rows of bottles lined up along the edge of the stage...

Hands on

I reckon this is a Gash Dit, but there is a little nagging bit which says it might, just might, be based on the truth?

I'll let you decide.

Stevie H and I on a lunchtime sesh with our mess oppos.

We were in Martha's, Portsmouth. If not, it was the Mucky Duck at the other end of town... anyway, which place it was does not really matter.

There was a group of girls sat at the next table. Thinking we could impress them we closed in and docked our arses around them.
As Jack does we started chatting to them, making up jobs and talking total shite.

Stevie K jabs a finger towards one of the girl's tits, his finger stops millimetre from poking her nipple as he announces he is the chief Bra sizer for Playtex.

He continues, bragging he can tell breast size simply by looking.

We sat back, waiting for him to dig himself into a hole with his gobshite.

The girls, however, seemed intrigued by his claim and challenge him to guess each of their sizes.

"You will have to lift your jumper, so I can see them properly," Steve says to the first girl. "It's more difficult to be accurate when thick knitwear is involved".

As good as gold, the girl peels her jumper from her torso until it is gathered around her neck like a woolly scarf. She then thrusts her breasts towards Stevie, for his inspection.

The rest of us shut the fuck up and just enjoyed watching like the voyeuristic perverts we were.

Not admitting it, but we were all reluctantly admiring Stevie for his bravado, especially as his head was now shadowed between this girls' ample bosoms.

"34C," he eventually said, his voice muffled by her exposed cleavage.

She answered, "Yes, your dead right".

Before any of us could say a word the second girl whipped her paps out, placed both hands on the table and lent forwards, her boobs jiggling inches from Stevie's eyes.

"And what do you say mine are?" she asked.

I know what I could to have said they were and what I would like to do with them. I am sure the other lads were thinking much the same thing... but that's another story I guess?

Stevie gave this girl's chest a good once over, a twice over and a thrice over, before saying "36D".

Smiling the girl sat down and began buttoning her puppies back into the blouse from whence they sprang.

"You have a good eye," she said, nodding at Stevie

"I have two good eyes'," was Stevie's instant retort.

I have to say he was on form and clearly relishing this activity, as were we all.

Stevie guessed the next two girl's sizes correctly.
I was wondering if he really practised this, or if he was just being an extremely jammy twat?

Which brings us to the last girl. A girl who sported a pair of mahoosive hooters.

With a tilt of her head and a wry smile she pulls her camy-top off, cups each boob with her hands and hoists those melons high.

"Come on then." She challenges Stevie, "How big are my twins?"

It was definitely said in a challenging way.

It was no secret Stevie liked big tits and now he was like a kid in a sweet shop, eyes almost popping out of his head, like in a Tom and Jerry cartoon.

Stevie moved from his chair to a bar stool and sat right in front of the girl.

"Yes," he said nodding sagely, "They are a good pair".

The cheeky bastard then said to the girl, to judge her size accurately he would need to feel their weight.

"That's fine," she said, flopping them into Stevie's open, outstretched and waiting palms.

Stevie did not require any further encouragement. He jiggled those twins about for a few minutes, bouncing them up and down a bit, together and one by one, before announcing "36DD".

The girl clapped her hands, grabbed Stevie's head and kissed him.
Unbelievably the jammy little bugger guessed all five of the girl's bra sizes correctly.

Proof that sometimes total bullshite and bollox works a treat.

It is also rumoured Stevie and Miss mahoosive hooters had a bit of a fling, until his next deployment.

Others say they got married... but then rumors are usually just rumours... aren't they?

Marsovin and Deck Polish

I recall one experience, courtesy of Malta, the Gut and Marsovin.

One night ashore I decided to stay on neat marsypops and not dilute it with the usual seven-up.

Bad move. The following morning, I puked in the mess square as soon as my eyes opened.

Although I cleaned the offending semi-liquid away, my lumpy vomit had eaten through the floor polish leaving the mess square with a large patch of lighter linoleum which would be questioned during rounds.

The mess killick was not happy. He made me spend the whole day scraping off the years' worth of accumulated old polish from the entire area.

I'm guessing there must have been twenty or thirty years of our mess's history in those layers.

Once every last inch of the old polish was removed and the surface of the original flooring was exposed to daylight, he the suggest I re-coat the deck with as many layers of ME7 as I could before the end of watch and themes began to fill up with my off-duty oppos.

I was just a 17-year-old kid.

This was a bit of a wake-up call.

I realized then, the three badge'rs in the mess did actually know more than I did when it came to pissing it up and local brews.

They told me it would end in tears at the start of the evening, I said they were too old to keep up with us young skins.

Of course, they were right.

It was the start of many happy days, about 7,300 of them.

Locked cock

A further tale about a stoker's tail

I was on watch in the control room. The boat on the surface, heading back to the UK.

Brian, who was not on watch, was in the after corner, where he was talking to another stoker, one who was working the hydraulic systems and masts from the panel in that corner. Brian and the Stoker had been in a deep discussion for almost an hour

I could see the discussion was becoming heated, the more so the longer it went on. I could not hear what was being said, but Brian was getting very agitated.

It was apparent that sooner or later a fight would break out and, as they were only a few feet from the Captain's cabin, I decided to see what I could do to calm things down.

They were face to face, in fact, you could say, nose to nose, as I stepped between them.

I asked, Brian "what are you doing here? You are off watch and you're making enough noise to wake the flaming dead. Get back to your mess and, whatever your gripe is, talk about it later." Which I thought was fair enough.

"But it bloody hurts like fuck and he won't tell me where it is," Brian replied.

"What hurts and what won't tell you where it is?" I asked.

"My knob hurts and he won't tell me where the fucking key is."
I admit I was struggling with this conversation. I had no idea what he was on about.

"Hang on, Brian. Tell me what is wrong, in clear English so I can understand what the hell you're waffling on about," I said.

I'll show you what I'm fucking on about," said Brian, dropping his kegs around his ankles and lifting his cock out so it lay in the palm of his hand.

"Look at that fucker," he said.

My eyes almost popped out of my head.

"Now, do you see what I mean?" he demanded.

Where Brian's gold cock ring previously lived, was a large, very strong, steel security padlock. I estimated it must weigh at least a pound. What's more, the bloody thing was stretching brian's foreskin until it almost touched his knees.

"The lads in the mess held me down, took my ring out and put this in its place." He said by way of explanation, "now the fucking fuckers won't give me the key to unlock the fucking bastard thing". Brian was now waving his arms about in frustration.

Unfortunately, at this very moment, the Captain come out of his cabin. Being disturbed by the raised voices he wanted to investigate.

The Captain was met by the sight of Brian, kegs around ankles and a shiny steel padlocked dangling from the end of his John Thomas.

He stare went from the padlock to Brian's face, to the other stoker and then to me, before returning briefly to Brian's dick.

"I don't want to know what this is about, but you and the Chief Stoker will make sure that this" (*pointing at Brian's family jewels*),"is sorted out forthwith, understood?"

"Yes sir," I replied. With a grunt the skipper returned to his cabin, shaking his head in wonderment.

"Brian, you are a fucking arsehole," I said, angry at being bollocked by the Captain.

"Dave, give him the key, and that's an order," I said harshly.

"No."

"I am not frigging messing about, if you don't give him the key, I will troop you for disobeying a direct order. Now, give him the key," I was beginning to lose it with Dave by now.

"I can't," he said.

"What do you mean, you can't. If it's in your locker, go and get it. If someone else has it, get them to give Brian the key, FFS."

"You don't understand. I can't give him the key, because I threw it over the side".

"You did what?" I was gasping in disbelief.

This was unbelievable.

Brian looked as though he was going to cry. He began to protest.

"What am I going to say to my wife when I get home with this on me dick? Sorry darling, I can't shag you 'til the fire brigade have cut this off me knob?"

I tried to calm him down.

"Brian", I said, "fuck off to your mess, I'll get the Chief and work out how to sort this. And you...." I turned to Dave but couldn't hold back the laughter any more.

I simply walked away, pissing myself laughing at the pathetic crap going on. The tears were streaming down my face.

The Chief Stoker and I retired to the heads to check out Brian's heavyweight jewellery.

The yellow 'marigold' style rubber gloves we wore to inspect the offending article made us look like demented doctors from a 'B' movie, as we turned it around and inspected it from all angles.

It was no ordinary padlock. It was tempered steel, the type used on the gun lockers. Its removal would not be an easy exercise.

The Chief Tiff was called to the inspection, who, in turn summoned the Engineering Officer.

It is amazing how many men decided they needed to visit the heads during the time it took to inspect Brains appendage.

By the time the 'umming' and 'arhhing' was over, things were getting serious for Brian's cock. It was turning a funny mottled blue with highlights of purple and going sort of blotchy. It was clear something had to be done PDQ.

"Brian," said the Chief Stoker, "the only way to get that out is to hacksaw the fucker off... the lock, not your dick I mean."

Brian nodded. The poor sod looked relieved.

"Alright, but do it quickly please, its really hurting now," he pleaded.

"I am not doing it. One I slip could slice your knob off. You'll have to do it yourself".

We assisted him into the engine room, as Brian was finding it difficult to walk. The engine room is the only place on the boat where there was a vice. It was slightly above waist height, between the back end of the engines.

Brian, standing on tiptoes, naked from the waist down, got the padlock into the vice his foreskin stretched like a very long elastic band,

Unfortunately for him, the sea was quite choppy. So, as the boat rolled, Brian needed to roll with it. However, his cock, firmly clamped in the vice, did not move very far.

Every time the boat rolled to port, Brian was forced farther away from the vice. Each time this happened he squealed like a stuck pig.

Now, Brian was hacksawing away for all he was worth but, as we all know, when you hacksaw metal it gets very hot. So, every now and then he had to stop and let the metal cool. Under 'normal' circumstances he could have poured some cold water onto the locks hasp, but as we were returning from quite a long stint at sea, there was no water to be had.

It took Brian almost an hour of stop/start sawing to release, almost an hour later. He, or his cock and surrounding area was burnt and blistered to buggery.

From the engine room, Brian made a bee-line for the docs for some salve and pain relief.

After such a painful event he never put his gold Albert ring back.

I have wondered what his wife said when he got home with a swollen, scarred penis with an extra, extra-large hole in the end?

Maybe he blamed it on the Albert? We may never know.

It is rumored that...

John C---- covered the skipper's carpet with cress seed, watering it well in before he left for his six weeks summer leave.

I am certain he would have won an Oscar for wearing such an expression of bewilderment on his face when he returned aboard and was subsequently questioned by the Joss.

Priceless.

HMS/M Otus

Gen

Falmouth Mid-Eighties

HMS/M Otus alongside, port side to.

On another jetty is the Pollington (*Ton class minesweeper for the sprogs*). The jetties in those days were wooden.

We are berthed ashore, which was standard practice back then, in a cheapo hotel when we decide on a DTS and why not!

We merrily trot to our adopted pub. There is a bunch of skimmers inside downing a bevy or three, no problem. Everyone was enjoying the day...

...until one of my WEM's lobs a load of 2p coins at them and says, "oye, you, skimmers, have a brew on my subsistence".

So, it kicked off.

I leapt in, trying to calm things down, suggesting that as It was only 14:00, we all, skimmers and deeps, meet up for a joint run ashore later that evening. For us, it would be the last run for a while, as we were sailing at 05:00 back to Dolphin.

So, there we are, waiting (*us lot had been in the British Legion all afternoon as the pubs were shut*) when the skimmers turned up on mass, all wearing togas.

Why the effing hell they were wearing togas, who knows, in fact, who cares?

Anyway, we were outdone, but a brill night of piss taking, dits and singing ensued. The night ended with yours truly leading a massed chorus of "My Way", sad but true.

Now, imagine it is 05:00, Harbour Stations.

Off we go, straight back to Pompey on the roof, none of the usual hassle of going past Portland. We arrive at Dolphin around 22:00.

At Dolphin, STARBOARD side to, trot 1, you could see from the jetty, in big white letters "WE DID IT OUR WAY, LUV POLLY," painted in bright whitewash alongside the casing. (Obviously, when you are on the casing or bridge you can't see it.)

We wondered what all the cross-channel ferries and shipping thought of that one.

I wish that was me

Gash

Scouse is sat in the forward heads and he can hear the

sound of running feet thumping through the ships steelwork from several deck's up.

The sound becoming continuously louder the closer to the heads they got.

The main door to the heads bursts open and Scouse hears someone rushing into the trap next to the one he is using.

"Oh, arghhh, yes... fucking hell..."

The words are accompanied by a backdrop of long, wet farts and the unmistakable squishing sound of the squits, followed by the usual acrid stench.

Being a bit on the constipated side, Scouse calls out, "Fuck me, mate. I wish that was me right now."

"So, the fuck do I," comes the reply, "I ain't even got me fuckin ovies off yet."

Painter Man

Bobby Trainter looked like the archetypal mad scientist, he rarely combed his hair, had paint spotted steel-rimmed glasses, 'Pussers grey' faded overalls (they were once navy blue) and of course, he was as daft as a brush.

Bobby lived in a man-cave under the fo'c'sle, called the paint shop, only venturing out for the occasional run ashore.

Most of Bobby's meals were brought to him by one of the Junior Seamen, who would push the scran under the door, then leg it just in case Bobby might invite him inside.

Bobby was a great bloke for a sods opera and he would be first in line whenever someone organized a piss-up and he hated brown hatters. But apart from that he did tend to keep to himself.

We thought it a bit strange when Bobby was one of the first ashore when we docked in New London, *Connecticut.* Because along with it being the US Navy's prime submarine base, it gained a reputation for being a poofter's paradise.

Some decided that Bobby had "Gone on a poofter culling run."

In the early hours of the morning, Bobby arrived back at the ship. The taxi driver pulled him from the backseat and dumped him on the jetty, where he was spotted by the Jimmy.

Bobby was absolutely legless, cap-less, speechless and as his breathing was shallow, so we got the Doc out of his pit to examine him. Bobby was turned in to the sick bay for the night.

Next day Bobby was put on defaulters. He still could not stand up straight, nor could he speak. He did mutter something about only two pints. Some guessed a brown hatter spiked his drinks!

By the time Bobby got to the Jimmys' Defaulters, he was somewhere near normal. Even if normal for Bobby's was quite an individual determination.

The Jimmy wore his steel-rimmed glasses at defaulters this enhanced his menacing appearance, a bit like Josef Göbbels. And I often wondered if they are related.

"Well, Mr Trainter", said the Jimmy, "I have the misfortune of witness your arrival back aboard, what do you have to say for yourself"?

"I don't know sir, I can't remember. I only had a few pints, but my memory is blank. That's the truth sir, I haven't been ashore for weeks since I left the last clinic."

"What clinic? What were you doing at a clinic?" asked the Jimmy, "and why didn't you mention it before now?"

"I'm a rare blood group sir and they pay good money over here for it."

"You mean to tell me, you gave a pint of blood before going on the piss?"

"Oh, no sir." said Bobby, "I gave two pints of blood, at two different places. They told me to drink plenty of liquid."

"I'm surprised you are still alive, Trainter", said the Jimmy. "Good God man, Captain's Report. Add self-inflicted injury to the charges Cox'n."

"I hope you have learned something today, Trainter."

"Oh, yes sir. Wiser and richer, wiser and richer."

Which went right over Jimmy's head.

Recuperation

Joke

Jack is lying in his hospital bed, wearing an oxygen mask over his mouth and nose. He is still heavily sedated from a four-hour, difficult, surgical procedure.

A young, student nurse arrives to give him a partial sponge bath.

"Nurse", Jack mumbles, from behind the mask. "Are my testicles black?"

Slightly embarrassed by the directness of Jack's question, the young nurse replies, "I don't know, Sir. I'm only here to wash your upper body and feet."

Jack raises his head slightly and asks again, "Nurse, are my testicles black?"

Concerned he may elevate his vitals from worry about his testicles, the nurse overcomes her nervousness and quietly pulls back the covers.

She pulls his gown up, lifts his penis in one hand and cups his testicles in the other. She takes a close look and says, "There's nothing wrong with your testicles, Sir"

Jack manages to pull the oxygen mask from his face.
He smiles at the nurse and says very slowly.

"Thank you very much. That was wonderful. But listen very carefully",

I asked you, "A r e - m y - t e s t - r e s u l t s - b a c k?"

Morning Blues

Monday morning, after a long weekend leave.

Meaning, I sodded off home ASAP after my watch ended on Thursday afternoon.

I am driving back to Guzz.

It is 04.30

I need to be ready for my morning watch as I was Breakfast cook in the wardroom galley.
My oppo, Buster, spent the weekend on the piss with me, was sitting in the passenger seat.

When those dreaded blue lights started flashing behind me. I checked my speedo, it read 120 MPH.

As the 'Fuzz', (*remember that word? Yes, this was in the Seventies!*) pulled me over, Buster said, "I was fucked."

He said I would lose my licence. Which would mean I would be in the shit with the Joss and get some 9's and fines and all that crap they put on you for *'bringing the Royal Navy into disrepute'.*

Anyway, the copper comes to my window, knocks on it and gestures for me to wind it down. (*Yep, 'wind' it down by turning a little handle round and round. There were no fancy electric motors in back those days.*)

"Do you know how fast you were going?" The cooper asks, poking his head into the car and taking a good look at us.

"Ummmm, about 65/75?" I say, lying through my teeth.

The copper looks at me, his eyebrows raise and his head tilts to one side.

I continue speaking, "The thing is, officer, we are Navy and our ship is sailing in 45 minutes. We will be in deep shite if we don't get back before then."

A wide grin spread across the coppers face. I glanced towards Buster. He was still as a statue, staring straight ahead, not even blinking.

"Fuck off you knob-jockey," the copper said, "I've only been out the Mob for 18 months. I did 22 years. If you're sailing at 05.15 in the morning, I'll shag my grandmothers' arse."

Buster's head jerked around and we glanced at each other for a fleeting second, knowing the cop had sussed my lie, Busters expression was one which said, 'I told you so'.

The cop continued speaking, "Now fuck off, but if I see you doing anything over eighty you will need a bloody big pair of wellies, you got me?"

I started nodded like a shite-ting whippet with whipcord and said, "thank you," at least twenty times.

I was still nodding five miles down the road when Buster heard my sphincter relax.

Where's my bike?

An abridged Submariners 'Gen dit'

Bermuda, circa 19... something or other.

Alongside Malabar, on Courageous.

Gathered subsistence from Ships Office. Got Bus to hotel (*The Bermudian*) in Hamilton.

Later that day I rented one of those *'Death Wish'* mopeds and made my way to the Bermuda Police Club where I got absolutely minging.

Decided to use the moped to assist my return to The Bermudian, as I was finding it difficult to stand upright without its aid.

I made it back safely; via the hotel's tennis courts and by driving through two fences, which I am sure were not there previously, several assorted flower beds and some sun beds.

I don't think the mopeds breaks were working very well which necessitated me parking the thing in the deep end of hotel swimming pool.

After which I swam ashore and headed to my hotel room, which some twat had moved.

I woke up on the Ice-Making machine in the passageway between the rooms, several hours later.

On climbing down from my makeshift bunk, I was desperately trying to recall where I'd left my moped.

Norfolk, Virginia, 1972

CONQUEROR just arrived and is about to give it some welly.

Unfortunately, hurricane whatever its name, followed us in and begins to blow up a good 'un.

The Skipper decides it would be wise to put out extra lines, so duty watch assembles and starts putting loads of lines across.

Our activities are being watched by the USN, from the safety of the jetty.

With waves washing over the after casing, all have dog leads on; but somehow the Scratcher, a chap called Ginge, manages to get himself overboard and is bouncing up and down the side, much to the amusement of the assembled hands, who are as wet under their foulies as is Ginge is flapping about in the 'oggin.

Unamused, the Skipper turns to OOD and says, "Ok, Mike, we've had our fun now, let's get the job finished."

Quick as a flash, Mike yells "When you've finished fucking around, Second Coxswain, could you come back inboard and give us a hand to finish getting these lines rigged? It's rather wet up here."

The Yanks nearly pissed their pants.

Anaywayhow, deservedly large tots of wardroom brandy all round for a warm-up, even for Ginge.

Khai

Here is another oldie.
This one, I am sure, having origins of truth.

An (*nameless*) officers Steward, used to take a mug of Khai onto the bridge each morning for the Jimmy, as he kept a standing morning watch.

This went on for some time, whatever the weather, whatever the sea conditions.

Each morning the Jimmy would be presented with a full mug of Khai.

One morning the Jimmy askes the Steward how, whatever the weather, he managed to get a cup, full to the brim of Khai, from the galley, along the passageways, up the steps and onto the bridge, without seeming to spill a single drop.

"Ahh, now", said the Steward, "That is a branch secret. One I am not a liberty to reveal to you. But, once we return home and I am going to my next draft, I shall reveal all to you".

No matter how many times the Jimmy asked during deployment, the answer was always the same.

Eighteen months later the Steward, kitbag over his shoulder is leaving for his next draft.

As he starts down the gangplank he hears the Jimmy calling him.

"Now, remember you promised to reveal your secret," he reminds the Steward.
"I remember my promise," he said.

"Tell me how you managed to get a full mug of Khai onto the bridge every morning for the past eighteen months without ever spilling a single drop," he asks of the Steward once again, eagerly awaiting the answer.

"Well", says the steward, "it is simple really. I fill the mug to the brim, take one great gulper and walk to the bridge as quickly as possible. Once I get there, I dribble the Khai I have safe in my mouth back into the mug and, 'hey presto' its full to the brim once more".

With that, he gives the Jimmy a wave and trots off to catch the train to Portsmouth.

In a Coma

Joke

Jack visits his wife, who is in a coma, in hospital. He has done so several years, hoping that one day she will wake.

As he is chatting away, his hand strays and he begins to fondle her right breast. His wife lets out a short sigh.

This is the first sound, the first reaction, she has made in all the years she has been confined.

Jack is so excited he runs to the doctor and tells him of her reaction.

"That is a good sign," says the doctor, suggesting that Jack try fondling her left breast, to see if anything happens.

Jack returns to his wife rubs her left breast. Which brings another moan from his wife.

He rushes back to the doctor.

The doctor thinks this is wonderful news. It could possibly be the breakthrough they were hoping for. So, he asks Jack if he would return to his wife and perform oral sex.

More than happy with the doctor's request, Jack once more goes back to his wife's bedside, this time to do the deed as suggested.

Five minutes later, Jack comes running up to the doctor looking agitated.

"What's going on?" asks the doctor.

Jack yells, "It's my wife. She has stopped breathing"

"What happened?" asks the doctor, "everything seemed to be going so well?"

Jack answered, "I think she choked on my cock."

It's a snip

A shaggy dog dit

I was married by the time I was 20 and like most randy matelots, produced a family at the double.

Our third daughter arrived by the time I was 30.

It was a difficult birth and, after discussions with my GP, I decided to do the decent thing and go for the snip.

It was mentioned having it done on the NHS involved a lengthy wait, whereas if I paid £25, I could have it done privately within days.
So, I paid my money to jump the queue

A week later, having shaved off ready for the op, I get in the car and set off to get the job done.

I lay on the table and this big, butch nurse walked in, gathered up my meat and two veg and remarked, "My, we have been a good boy, now don't worry, this won't hurt."

And guess what... it did not.

After the op, I get back in the car and drove home, where I asked the boss what time scran would be ready and she told me it would be another hour or so.
Reading my mind, she said as I'd been a good boy today, I could go and have a couple of wets with my oppos.

So, off I trott.

There I am, standing at the bar swinging the lamp for all it's worth when the pain hits me like a donkey kicking me straight in the bollocks.

If ever they tell you going for the snip doesn't hurt, you wait until the anaesthetic wears off.
It hurts like a fucking fucker fucking a fucker

Of course, my oppos being sympathetic types, carried on drinking while I'm rolling about in agony on the pub floor trying to cradle what's left of my bits and bobs.

It was three days before the pain subside to the degree that I could breathe naturally.

The moral of this story is, never believe what they tell you on the operating table, it's all bullshit.

Miss H. H

This, I am informed is a gen, gen dit.
If it is, we have another legend walking among us.

An un-nameable Jenny, (*sorry, female sailor*), sneaked a hired moped onto the Invincible.

She managed, single handed-ly, (*she swears she did not have help, or accomplices, of either gender aiding her*), to get the moped onto the flight deck.

Revving the little machine and winding back the throttle, she drove the entire length of the flight deck, up the ski-ramp and got airborne... for a millisecond.

On landing, thankfully ditching the moped before hitting the 'oggin, the impact nearly tore her in half.

Doc L administered 11 sutures and prescribed posture and light duties until her coccyx healed as best as could be expected.

She is still extremely grateful to Doc L for not dropping her in the shit.

Legend you are, Miss H. H.

(The Unnameable Jenny...lady sailor, jack-ess... or is that Jack-ass?)

Paddy's ferry

Another Deeps dit

J ust before I joined *(an un-namable boat),* it is off Ireland and the skipper decides to bring her up for a look about.

Up to 120ft all quiet, periscope depth, up they go, scope and other masts going up.

BANG.

Right into an Irish ferry, which is sat, for some reason, with everything switched off so it was not detected.

The ferry skipper, hearing an almighty clang and feeling his ship lift a couple of feet, realises what it is and sends a signal, saying he has just been hit by an unknown submarine.

"Shit," think the grownups. They panic and send out the fleet, Nimrods, other boats, the full Monty.

Meanwhile, this boat has gone deep and is legging it.

At daft o'clock it surfaces and the wrecker is sent up onto the fin with a sledgehammer, to try and get the bends out of the masts so they can get them down.

He also removes a large chunk of ferry propeller he found stuck in the fin.

I have had a few arse tighteners in boats, but I'm glad to say I missed that one.

In short...

H ands up who can spin a dit regarding "Diamond Lil's

show bar" in union Strasser, or the Bistro nite spot in sunny Southsea. Club Albane (TheMighty Fine) Pompey, or for those a little older how about the "Hotel Lennor," (Lennox) again Pompey.

For those ladies and Gentlemen of the sea who remember "The Black Angus" San Juan, it is this watering hole I wish to discuss.

Back when I was a young piece of skin and essence, I found myself with a group of messmates, all fine fellows indeed, sampling Large volumes of the local brew, when my keen if not slightly blurred vision, fell upon a lovely young lady sat at the bar
I approached Said dusky maiden and after a little discussion, agreed on a price of $5 American.

All night in.

I was chuffed with my bargain bit of haggling
And turned to my fellow chefs, to give my farewells.

On returning to my vision of loveliness I discovered why she was a bargain.

She had suffered from polio at birth and couldn't walk, she had to drag herself orangutan stile, across the floor.

The rest is all blurred!

Jack & the big purple one

Dit

few years back, myself and one of my bezzie oppos from Raleigh, were reunited for a course at HMS Collingwood.

Having not seen Jack, (*that really is his name*), for quite some time, as he had gone off to be a sun dodging sludgemariner, we decided a piss up was on the cards.

We started at a Wetherspoons in Fareham and, before too much ale was consumed, we found ourselves talking to a couple of fairly attractive student types.

Now, Jack has a strong Jockanese accent and the girls were finding this very sweet and sexy. Before long we managed to invite ourselves to a party the following evening.

We promised to meet them at their place the next day. Thereafter Jack and I proceeded on an un-eventful sesh, a few pints, watch the footy, kebab etc.

The following evening, Jack and I donned our best pulling shirts, applied the Joop in a liberal manner and headed over to the girl's place to seal the deal.

On arrival, we were greeted by a couple of suspicious looking student lads, long hair, ripped jeans, mummy and daddy paying their way, you know the sort. These two lads could clearly see we were a threat and were probably planning to trap off with our birds.

Anyway, the party was tame, with a sink full of cheap lager and a cd player knocking out some obscure crap these lads had put on. Not the huge clungefest we had been expecting.

After an hour or two of listening to the girls rabbiting on about Big Brother or something, Jack decided it was time to liven up the proceedings somewhat.

He went upstairs while I entertained the girls with a couple of my best salty sea dits. A few minutes passed before Jack re-appeared, wearing one of the girl's underwear over his clothes and with the biggest purple dildo I have ever seen sticking out of his flies.

Now this thing wasn't your run of the mill, rocket-shaped, vibrator. Oh no, this monster had flashing lights and was wobbling around violently, like some sort of serpent. The thing had some serious motors inside. It sounded like a hedge strimmer.

The girl who it belonged to went bright red and burst into tears, while one of the student lads, like a knight in shining armour, rose to defend his maiden's honour.

After a stiff telling off and threats of violence from the youth, Jack could take no more from the jumped-up little prick and sparked him clean out with a quick left hook.

We decided it was time to leave, made our excuses and walked out, Jack still wearing the underwear and holding his prize aloft like a sporting champion.

From time to time we would see the same girls around town, but they never wanted to chat for some reason.

Losing it

As Navigators Yeoman on a certain boat, one of my mundane tasks was to ensure a plentiful supply of 2B pencils for chart work, CEP etc. as they are easy to erase.

I soon learnt that all and sundry nick the pencils off the chart table, so as well as 2B pencils, I would indent for a large supply of HB pencils for the troops.

A tickler tin full of HB pencils, masking taped to the end of the chart table, was the ready supply locker for distribution of the said troops pencils.

Of course, there was always the lazy bastards, the ones who could not be bothered to pick up the correct pencil and just grabbed the first one they saw on the chart table.

After a long fish play exercise, (*during which I had little sleep, as after all those 'attacks' I had to prepare the records, so spent more time on watch than off.*) I found we had just about exhausted the current supply of 2B pencils.

Being a happy young soul, I grab a wad of HB pencils and begin to amble through the boat, swapping one for one, new HB for old 2B, getting all the Widow Wanky and 'to be or not to be' jokes as I go.

In the stoker's mess back aft, one of the young stokers is writing numbers on some form of stokery record sheet.

I ask for my 2B pencils, offering HB in exchange, a couple of lads pass over pencils.
But young stokes, who is obviously using a 2B pencil, (I have a trained Navs eye for these things), just blanked me.

So, I politely ask for said pencil.

"Fuck off" came the reply.

The red mist did not just come over me, it fell like a 10-ton weight about my being.

Instantaneously, I was across the table, holding the young stokes by the throat, trying to push the said pencil firmly up his Harris, all the way up, so I could drag it out of his snot locker.

His messmates eventually managed to drag me off and shuffled me for'd.

About an hour later, the Killick of the aft mess came forward and invited me, the Killick of the forward mess, back aft, for gulpers from a young stoker and maybe a bit of sippers.

OK! YES, I went back aft!

(*That's about the only time I can remember losing it while at sea*).

Some 'on watch' training

W e were heading South, across the equator, so the sprogs could cross the line and get bummed by Neptune.

The usual fun and games were had during the ceremony and one of the bears (the PWO) got a particularly rough shoeing down the dabber's mess for some reason, resulting in a black eye.

Anyway, it was all fun and games.

Unfortunately, I had the middle on the bridge that night. So, after pissing it up all day, I got my head down for 45 mins before turning to on the bridge totally hammered.

As luck would have it, the Officer of the watch and QM were also pissed, so we all just sat there in silence, not wishing to incriminate one another.

At some point, I must have drifted off, because the next thing I recall is waking up at the wheel and noticing I'd knocked the autohelm off.

The ship was a good 20 degrees off course.

In a panic, I looked around and saw the OOW zonked out in the skipper's chair and the QM nowhere to be seen (*he was racked out under the comma console*).

The ship had literally been adrift for a good 20 mins or so, with the entire bridge team asleep.

Realising I had got away with it, I slowly corrected our course before subtlety waking up the OOW.

He checked the chart and realised we may have taken a little detour, as he proceeded to bollock me, the QM appeared with the immortal line, *"We were just doing some on watch training."*

Nothing more was said.

A few days later we docked in Chennai. (*Madras*)

Navigators

Gash

Whand Sea Vixens first entered service onboard the

Navy carriers in 1964 many pilots were unhappy because they would have to fly with navigators.

One young pilot was moaning in the wardroom.

A veteran pilot overheard him, saying "You shouldn't be running down the navigator's son, I owe my life to one. We ditched in the desert miles from anywhere, no food, only a little water and the sun was merciless"

"What did your navigator do?" asked the young pilot, "lead you back to civilisation?"

"No," said the veteran, "I ate him!"

My oppo...

Yeah, right.... Gash dit

My Oppo said he was on the focsle of a type 23, when

at specials.

A great big goffer hit the ship and with it, a dolphin landed on the deck.

My oppo picked up the dolphin up and threw it back over the side.

As the dolphin was in mid-air, just before it fell back into the sea, my oppo swears it turned around and winked at him, as if to say, "cheers shippers".

Van & Scran

Gen dit

W ay back in the distant past, well, 1966 to be exact.

I was one of the watch-keepers in the Ground Radio Station at Camel Hill, adjacent to the main A303 road, about three miles from RNAS Yeovilton.

Because it needed to be manned 24/7, our routine was 24 hours on and 24 hours off.
This meant running our own fully-equipped galley, which was victualed from the air station down the road.

One night, realising we were running low on fresh scran, the duty PO threw me the keys to the Bedford van and ordered me to drive to Yeovilton. He said to get some steaks, joints of beef and a few veggies along with bacon and eggs for breakfasts.

I told him I couldn't drive and did not have a licence.

He said, "Don't fucking argue, now's the time to learn. Go on, piss off. I'm getting my head down."

So, there I was in a massive military Bedford truck at 03:00 hrs kangarooing down the A303 towards Yeovilton.

Luckily, I soon got the hang of things and at that time of night, there was fuck all traffic about, unlike nowadays.

After that incident, I volunteered to drive the van whenever I could, which gave me loads of practice before I eventually took my driving test.

Yep, somethings were really much better back then.

Happy Days, indeed.

South Africa

I got forced into taking 14 days Station leave with a South African farmer and his wife.

The Joss thinks it's frigging hilarious, shipping me off into lion territory.

When we get to the farm, 30,000 hot, dusty and torturous frigging miles from nowhere, bingo, the farmer has two young daughters.

One I learn is 16, the other just turned 19.

I know, this sounds like a bad joke, but stick with me...

On the first morning, the youngest girl hands me a rifle, a box of ammo and tells me we are going swimming.

The pool, she says, is about one and a half miles in a straight line directly from the front door of the farmhouse.

We set off walking to the pool.

In the long grass of the bush is a small hollow, the hollow holds the so-called pool, which is just a natural pond.

We go swimming, skinny dipping, which inevitably leads to us playing bury the snake.

The next day we are in the sitting room and I have my hand under her, a finger firmly inserted, when Dad comes in.

He cannot see the state of play, so starts yapping about woodwork.
After about an hour, all feeling has left my hand and the pain in my wrist is becoming unbearable.
Luckily, Mom calls us for big eats and we follow him into the kitchen.
I can only just grip my fork, as my hand is still numb.

The older sister comes to the rescue when she sees me struggling to cut my food.

While she is cutting my food for me, she detects the scent of fanny on my hands. Our eyes only met for a millisecond, but it is enough to confirm her suspicions.

During the rest of the mealtime, she makes many double entendre comments, which, luckily, go way over the heads of the girl's parents.

When we are sat on the porch after dinner, she makes me a direct offer, one which I could not possibly refuse.

I still had ten days leave to go.

I fucking love that Jossman!

The moped and the missing Chris

While was on a course at Collingwood, I bought a moped which I used to use for buzzing around Pompey and impressing 16-year-old girls with. It was great fun and gave me some freedom away from the base.

One of the lads on my course was going through a bit of a rough patch. He rented a flat in Gosport, where he lived with his wife and kid, but he did not have commuting to Collingwood each morning.

He slept on the base whenever he could not get home but was shit scared if he was found he would lose his LOA, which he relied on to help pay his rent.

The kid had clearly bitten off more than he could chew, which was why he was skint all the time.

Against my better judgement, I leant him my moped and helmet for a few months, so he could get to the base and back home again.

To be honest, although I liked and enjoyed the bike, I didn't really need it, so it was no real hassle for me to do without for a while.

A few months passed and he was looking after the bike well, he kept it clean and saw it was serviced and what not.

With my deployment coming up, it seemed like a logical step to sell it. I offered it to lad first, but he didn't have the cash.

Anyway, I struck a deal with another oppo, let's call him Billy, who bought the bike for £500.

He gave me £500 quid cash for the bike. I give him the V5 and the lad's number, so he could go and get the bike from him.

It was all a bit of a rush for me, as my deployment was brought forward a few weeks.

Both the lad and Billy are at Collingwood, but they didn't know each other at the time. However, I arrange for them to meet, so the bike can be handed over.

I fuck off on a 9-month deployment, assuming the two have met and the bike is now in Billy's possession.

Fast forward 9 years... yep, that's right, 9 years.

I receive a message from Billy, saying he is going to kill me unless I give him back the £500 quid he gave me for the moped, plus he want's interest on that money.

WTF?

Apparently, the handover never happened.
Every time Billy tried to contact the lad, he didn't answer. Billy tried to trace him through the mob, but his search was fruitless.

The lad just seemed to disappear into thin air.

Anyway, he had gone and so was the bike.

Billy placed the responsibility for this in my lap. Why he never reported the bike as stolen at the time, is beyond me.

Whatever, the fact is it seems I owe Billy £500 quid, plus nine years interest, because some scrote fucked off with the bike while I was on deployment.

It's a bit late to contact the old bill now!

So, if you know who the lad is let me know, because I need to get some money off the cunt.

Pembroke

Defo a Gen dit

I witnessed this myself.

Back in 1973, most trainee cooks knew the shortcut out of Pembroke.

A quick hop up the bank to where the lower rivet was removed from the railings and 'hey presto', one of the upright bars swung left or right, opening a gap large enough for most young men to slip through unhindered.

This enabled the junior rates to leave East Camp and the base without going through the main gate. More importantly, allowing them to return without the sentries or the Joss seeing them, whatever time of day or night or wee early morning hours, it might be.

There is a rumour that one day, a certain group of baby sailors were seen to enter this shore base by such a surreptitious route and such a security breach was reported to the MOD police.

Now, why this was reported to them and not to the Pembroke duty gate staff remains a mystery... so I am told.

The outcome was a MOD plod Landrover appeared on the scene and began to chase the suspects, who scattered in several directions.

Turning a corner, the said Landrover collided with a very large wooden cable reel which 'suddenly appeared' in the centre of the road on a blind bend.

Due to the relative low speed of the patrol vehicle, the only real and lasting damage was to the egos of the MOD police personnel.

It is said, even after making a series of visits, one to each of the Nissan huts which served as the trainee junior rates accommodation, the MOD plods left none the wiser as to whom they may have been pursuing.

The offending section of fence was re-joined to the lower support rail and remained so for a period of, oh, about a day.

Now, I had best make one last thing clear:

This available 'gap' in said fence was never used to sneak females into camp, especially on the night that the radio one roadshow arrived on the base.

Just saying.

Pills

Gen

While in the mob, I was given some pills from the doc,

for my total lack of interest and couldn't give a shit attitude.

I think nowadays they call it depression? Back then it was referred to as 'NAFFI'

The pills came in one of those small, dark green tablet bottles.

The handwritten label read, "Take 2 tablets a day. You will soon be springing around like a marine in a gay bar, in no time".

Noddy bags

Froggy French was confined to sick bay on the Ark Royal

in 1966, while she was on Far East duties.

The Doc's, sloping off, got him to dish out the 'Noddy Bags' (*now simply referred to as condoms I believe*), to all those going ashore who wanted them.

As Froggy was confined to his pit in the sick bay and could not go ashore, the twat pin-holed the entire box of 240 packets.

Now, who's the Daddy?

Drip Dry

Joke

Ralph and Edna were both patients in a mental hospital. One day while they were walking past the hospital swimming pool, Ralph suddenly jumped into the deep end. He sank to the bottom of the pool and stayed there.

Edna promptly jumped in to save him. She swam to the bottom and pulled him out.

When the Head Nurse Director became aware of Edna's heroic act she immediately ordered her to be discharged from the hospital, as she now considered her to be mentally stable.

When she went to tell Edna the news she said, 'Edna, I have good news and bad news. The good news is you're being discharged since you were able to rationally respond to a crisis by jumping in and saving the life of the person you love... I have concluded that your act displays sound mindedness.

The bad news is, Ralph hung himself in the bathroom with his bathrobe belt right after you saved him. I am so sorry, but he's dead.

Edna replied, 'He didn't hang himself, I put him there to dry.

How soon can I go home?'

Prolapse

I have no idea how true, or not, this dit is.

The grammar of the original left much to be desired, but the base language and narration gave the story a rather magical voice, especially when regarding the topic.

Whilst I have re-written the entire dit, I have stayed as true to the original as possible, to keep the rawness of the narrator's storytelling, much as it would have been relayed in the Mess.

I have a fat-arsed oppo who always squats over the pan when taking a shite.

The reason he does so is, some time back the sweaty bastard went for a plop, his big chunky cheeks drooped over the sides of the bowl, creating an air-tight seal. The gormless fucker goes to heave himself back onto his feet when the fat hanging from his elbow, like a greasy Sembawang sausage, hits the flusher.

Now, my oppo is wobbling around like a fucking Manatee on heat, whilst squealing like a seal out clubbing, because the enormous vacuum from the heads has sucked his ring-piece inside out like a meatloaf party popper.

Before you could shout 'prolapse', mongo chops is having a spasm. His arse looking like a shed load of spag-boll breakdancing across the deck on the back of a pig.

Hearing the screams coming from the trap, two of his oppos try and lift the portly penguin, but cannot, because of the cramped space in the heads and the size of the fat fucker himself.

Whilst attempting to lift him to his feet, they are also fighting the prevailing stench emanating from the exposed, inside-out, rippling intestine of porky's guff.

Braving it out, the fat bastards two oppo's dragged the porcine lump, along the gangway to the sickbay, on his belly, rewarding onlookers with a sight they shall never be able to un-see and a trail of smelly, slimy shit, marking the path of the journey.

No big eats

W hen tied up in Guz, we got the opportunity to go on

the smash. It was a nice change from Pompey.

Invariably we would end up in the Avondale or the Keyham, both of which boasted topless barmaids.
Most of the barmaids had rather questionable looks, at least for the first several pints or so. After which, they all became surprisingly desirable.

One evening, a half-eaten kebab was left in one of the flats on 2 Deck. It got picked up on daily rounds by a FOSTY and by way of punishment, the Jimmy banned the consumption of any big eats onboard.

Every night for the next two weeks all the takeaways in Plymouth arrived at the gangway to delivered unwanted feasts for the XO.

I ordered him cheesy chips and deep-fried black pudding along with a large bottle of coke.

Eventually he cracked, allowing us to order big eats if we promised not to make a mess.

Unfortunately, by the time he capitulated, not one take away in the entire city would deliver to HMS Exeter anymore.

Shame!

Un-politically correct

(Even back then.)

This is harsh and I wondered if I should share it at all?

But then, I got all philosophical and thought, fuck it.

So, here it is.

I t was told to me by a chap I shared an office with, in my final job before retirement.

Aboard (*the old*) HMS Bulwark. Whilst in Hamburg, circa. 1969.

My office colleague was the Officer of the Patrol. Which was called out to a disturbance in a bar.

It is a small bar, a local's hangout and defo not a place for tourists, which is why Jack was there.

The place had a central dance floor. I say dancefloor, but the single spotlight shining down from the ceiling illuminated the entire wooden floored area.

I am sure are familiar, or have at least visited such places?

It turns out Jack arrived in this bar, slung his cap so it landed on the spotlight and asked, in a very loud voice

"Which of you Jew-burning bastards is going to buy me a beer?"

Hence the requirement for shore patrol.

The Truncheon

T he old bold boat, Truncheon is beating her way down a choppy English Channel on a surface passage to Faslane, when a large lump of timber, assisted by a goffer, re-designs our nice stretched aluminium sonar dome.

Shortly after this incident, the 1st Lt announces we are to make a short stop in Guzz, to collect a replacement fibreglass dome.

Sunday morning, we berth in Guzz dockyard, tiffies with tools start to gather on the casing.

Our Captain, Lt Cmd. R*** says to the Coxswain "Pipe lunch time leave, 12 noon to 2 pm."

A cheer echoes through the boat, tots are quickly downed. The new baby chef is told he will have to manage Sunday dinner, for the few on duty who will be left onboard.

Most of the crew hit the Avondale, Keyham Vaults etc.
2.30 pm. Three junior rates are adrift.

The skipper and most sober of the casing party are on the casing, when a Leading Patrolman appears with a handful of papers.

Lt Cmdr. R*** appears to be the only person of authority, so the L/Patrolman snaps him one off and says;

L/P "These are for you sir"

Capt. "What are they?"

L/P "Patrol reports of your crew this lunchtime sir."

Capt. "What do you want me to do with them?"

L/P "You will have to deal with them sir."

Lt CRMD, R*** then tears them up and lobs them into the harbour.

Capt. "There we are hooky, they are dealt with."

Aa a rather bemused L/Patrolman walked back ashore the casing party somehow manage not to cheer or give the skipper a round of applause.

But our brave but Captain calls out...

"Hooky, I am missing three Junior Rates. They are in uniform and have HM Submarine cap tallies. If you find them, could you post them to Faslane?"

As we sailed out of Guzz it is said that standing on the Hoe, were three "Jack-me-Ticklers" in full uniform, waving as we passed. Although the story goes, they were too far away to see if we're wearing HM Submarine cap tallies, or not.

I was later told the three, waving matelots later jumped into a fast black to the station, where they purchased three single tickets to Faslane.

Around and around the ragged rock...

...ran the rat-arsed Signalman

The Galatea was alongside in Gibraltar.

We were celebrating someone's birthday, I cannot remember whose. I may have well been my own?

Our run ashore plan was simple; down a few whets, go to the casino and win a few bob. Spend that few bob on a few more whets. Grab some big eats before downing a few more whets. Find a late bar and have a few more whets.

There were about six of us in the casino, all trying to look a cool as James Bond, but standing out like a bunch of Jacks' on a run ashore.

I put a pound on black nineteen, the sort of girl I fancied ending the night in, and it came up.

One of the other lads won on a red fourteen, I won't go into why he placed that bet.

Anyway, we were quid's in. I think between us we walked away about a ton up.

So, we headed down town to get rat-arsed on our winnings.

About 00.30, halfway through The Dance of the Flaming Arseholes, just about to light the paper, the fucking Redcaps came along.

One I recognized, he nicked me on a previous visit for feeding one of those bastard shitting Apes a few cans of Watney's Red Barrel.

Well, that same Redcap came right for me, so I dived out the bar window wearing just my knicks and flipflops.

Of course, the bloody Redcaps Landrover caught up with me, they can go faster than a (mostly) naked sailor in dodgy honky-fid flop-flips.

I did shout "Help, rape, help me, rapists" when they cornered me down a dead end.
But no assistance arrived.

In my head, this was like a scene from a Clint Eastwood movie just before he gets the drop on them spaghetti cowboy 'baddies.
There were three bloody great Redcaps facing poor little me, dressed in me kegs and trying to wriggle my foot back into the flipping-flopper which had a blow-out as I rounded the last bend.
The whole scene illuminated by the Landrover's headlamps.

Deciding it really was shite or bust for me, I ran straight at them, a couple of slinky like body swerves and I was past the lot of them.
Up I went, straight over the Landrover's bonnet, bounced along the cloth roof and 'orf along the raod shouting 'Freedom, freedom for Tooting', (remember Wolfie Smith?), straight into the arms of the Naval Patrol and the Provost Marshall.

Oh, shite.

It was one of the Bessie runs I had in Gib... ever.

Two Pence

Defo an Gash-un

An *'old oppo of mine'* was having a crafty blueliner in one of the boat bays on the Ark Royal.

Lounging against the bulkhead, he was playing with a two pence piece, flicking in in the air and catching it again.

As my old oppo became more confident, the higher he flicked the coin, until the time he tossed it so high, a gust of wind took it over the side.

Expecting to hear a faint 'plop' as the coin hit the 'ogging. My old oppo was shocked to hear a metallic 'tinging' noise instead.

Wondering what could have caused that noise, my old oppo took a shufty over the side, only to see a Russian Akula class Submarine beginning to disappear beneath the waves.

Just before it went under, my old oppo swears he saw the skipper give him a wink and a quick salute, before closing the hatch.

...and if you believe that...

Straight out of Barrow

O n a new boat, straight out of Barrow.

For about 10 minutes, about the time the machinery was switched over, there was a lot of noise and rattling.

The UC`s were chasing all over the boat checking for noise, shorts, broken mounts etc.

It got that bad, they were thinking of doing a scram and RC entry and checking in there.

The CHOPS was using the rack in the upper SR`s bunk space, the other side of the bulkhead from the sound house, so if it came up again, they could bang on the wall and he could leg it.

The noise reappeared, they banged on the bulkhead.

CHOPS legged it down the ladder by 29, turned down 2 deck said, "*out of the way*" as he pushed passed Ginger, the baby 29 watchkeeper... and stopped dead in his tracks.

"What the fuck are you doing, Ginger?" asks CHOPS.

"Practicing my tap-dancing chief," says Ginger.

Later that watch a sign appears, "NO TAP DANCING ON 2 DECK".

Shit faced

Officer of the Day, HMS York, Rosyth.

Some of the grunters went on a run ashore in Edinburgh.

So off down Rose street, they trundled.

Some jockenese porridge wog hears the piggies accents and slips a crippler drug cocktail into DWEOs wet, 10 minutes later he goes fucking bulgy eyeballed, sweaty and starts to shake like a shite-ting dog.

Before the rest of the grunters could stop him, he was out the boozer and legging it up the street.

DWEO WA, who fancied himself as a bit of a Bear Grylls type, zombie apocalypse survivor type chap, mainly because of all those survival types, boy's own, keep fit brown hatter type shite magazines he read.

This is a fucking freezing, Jockanesse land November night and, for whatever reason, in his drug-addled mind, our 'first blood DWEO decides he should take off all his clothes off and hide.

Ten marine minuets in some Edinburgh back alleyway, totally starker's, he recalls an article he read in one of those outdoor, survivalist, gung-ho, magazines.

Following the recalled instructions from said periodical, the DWEO takes an enormous dump and curls one off, smearing his entire body with his fresh shit, believing it would form an airtight seal around his skin and help retain his bodies heat.

Someone raised the alarm, either from the stench or seeing a shite covered figure diving in and out of the cities back streets.

The Police arrive, quickly and thankfully, passing him over to the Naval Provost.

Now, as the OOD I get a phone call at 23:30, from the Provost Marshall.

As I am only a CPO, the Provost Marshall says he needs to speak to an officer, immediately.
I inform him they are all on a run ashore.

After a pause, he says, "Chief, I suggest you clear the flight deck area and I only want you at the gangway."

Twenty moments later appears a shit covered, naked DWEO escorted by two crushers and the PM.

Still groggy with drugs, he smiles at me. As he does the dried crap cracks and he says, "Sorry, Smiffy."

PM says to get him showered, into his bunk and to tell no one, except the XO and MAA tomorrow.

Yeah right. Of course, I would keep this top secret.

Like fuck.

Who would pass a up the chance of spreading this news?

The whole of the ship's company knew the whole story come breakfast time.

Poor DWEO, who, by the way, seemed to leave the ship rather quickly after that incident.

They say he was urgently required on some shore base in the UK.

Shame, he was a really nice bloke.

Slipping in the back door

Gen

We were due to get a bonus for being away from our home port for so long.

The good old admiralty, being what they are, decided a weekend in Guz, on the way up to Northern Europe, would be a good idea, as it would stop us getting our bonus.

Not everyone had qualified (wardroom), so we were all miffed and the general attitude went a bit ROMFT.

I booked myself a hotel for the weekend and, as usual, ended up in the mighty Jesters on the first night, where I met a 'nice young lady'.

We went back to the hotel where we were going at it hammer and tong.

She is bent over the bed and in the throes of passion when the old man slips out.

Not wanting to let go of her ample boobs, I thrust forward sliding back inside at full steam ahead but it slips up recreation avenue

Well, she shot across the bed like a scolded cat, landing in a snotty heap and burst into tears.

Now, being the gentleman, I am, all I could do was piss myself laughing.

In a few moments we were back at it, so we could finish what we started.

Having a chat and a fag after I learned she worked for the child support agency... maybe I should have stayed knocking on the back door after all?

Tuk Tuk's & Delhi belly

Chennai (AKA Madras) Gen.

The place is a real eye-opener. It's bloody mental.

I have never seen anything like it before, or since.

I was almost decapitated as we began to tie up. One of the tugboats lines snapped. Fuck me it was awesome.
It was a stern line and left a great big dent in the bulkhead about on foot in front of where I was standing.

If I was one step closer My head would have been rolling about the deck, I kid you not.

The remainder of the rope fused to the bollard through friction.

Anywayhow...

From the instant the ship pulled alongside to the moment we left, beggars and feral street children smothered the dockside, ambushing any unsuspecting matelot going ashore.

Even ditching the gash was an epic event.

As you got to the bottom of the gangway a fecking great swarm of kids would rip the gash from your hands, tearing it to pieces and fighting over every last bit of shite.

In seconds it would be gone, every last potato skin, rust flake, or shitty scrap of old ncwspapcr.

I watched with astonishment as a malnourished teenage girl, single-handedly, dragged away the fucked tow rope which separated from the tug almost beheading me.

It took three of our lads to ditch it, but one scrawny little sod to drag it off into the netherworld where they live.

Madras was brilliant in other ways though.

We raced tuk-tuks along the streets, saw a dead man rotting in the dockyard and watched as people stepped over him, no one dare touch the corpse, because if they did they would become responsible, or so I am told.

I got naked in a 5-star hotel, ate the hottest and most disgusting tasting curry ever. A couple of lads were involved tuk-tuk crash. I think the driver lost some fingers.

Surprisingly there weren't more crashes as the roads are lethal, and for a few ickies, the tuk-tuk drivers would let you steer the bloody thing, even if you were pissed as a fart.

We had some James Bond style chases, people jumping out of the way as we raced down shit filled streets honking the horns and shouting, as we weaved between vehicles, pedestrians, dogs, rats, pile of crap, kids, handcarts and other tuk-tuk's.

We all got Delhi belly from the filth and shite though, which put a downer on the whole trip and soon all grew tired of the place.

Most of the ship's company spent the next two weeks shitting, many passing blood

I lost well over a stone during the time I was ill.

I recommend that any fat fucker who wants to shed a bit of podge should spend at least week in one of the big Indian cities.

The poverty is unbelievable.

This trip was an eye opener as to the psyche of the matelot, we can be reckless arseholes, obnoxious and bloody dangerous, but frigging good souls too, especially to your oppos.

Those were happy days.

The £40K Ring

Joke (probably)

An older white-haired gentleman walked into a jewellery store one evening recently with a beautiful much younger gal at his side. He told the jeweller he was looking for a special ring for his girlfriend.

The jeweller eyed him for a few seconds then looked through his stock and brought out a $5,000 ring.

The man said, 'No, I'd like to see something more special.' The jeweller happily dug to his special stock and brought another ring over.

"Here's a stunning ring at only $40,000" - the jeweller said. The young lady's eyes sparkled and her whole body trembled with excitement.

The old man seeing this said, 'We'll take it.'

The jeweller asked how payment would be made and the man stated,

'By check. I know you need to make sure my check is good, so I'll write it now and you call the bank Monday to verify the funds; We'll pick the ring up Monday afternoon.'

On Monday morning, the jeweller angrily phoned the man and said 'Sir...There's no money in that account."

"I know,' the man responded...

'But let me tell you about my weekend.'

You can learn a lot from older guys.

Stormy Portland

I trapped a nice little blonde waitress in a bar, in Portland during work up.

Somehow, I ended up lived in her flat, but she was always skint and I kept giving topping up the 'leccy meter, because it was fucking freezing without the fire, and bailing her out with a few quid each week.

I had this particular weekend off, so I took the bint for a DTS.

While on this DTS, it starts blowing a like a bastard outside, so I think, fuck this for a game of soldiers, I'm not going back to that freezing cold flat, I'll take her back to the POs mess for some bevvies.

Manchester was berthed on pier Q if I recall correctly. But with the wind blowing so hard we could barely stand upright it was taking some time heading in that direction.

As we get near the end of pier Q, I noticed she has a load of people on her deck.

It did not take long for me to sus she was at harbour stations.

(I later found there was a general recall, she was sailing to avoid the weather. I was PO of the Focsle by the way.)

I was that pissed, I thought fuck it, I'm not going back onboard if the fucker going out to sea, it's Saturday for fuck's sake.

A quick about turn and the bint and I got blown back to her gaff for the night, where I found a way to keep warm and out of the wind.

I snuck back onboard when Manchester came alongside the next day.

I almost shat myself when the killick POS told said he saw me and the bint legging it down the pier.

Good on him to keep schtum and well worth a queenies at Tot time for a couple of days.

Submariners will understand

Gen

It was in Stavanger, Norway.

The boat the Upholder.

We had to blow shit overboard, to a tanker.

The jetty was awash with fanny.

Finished.

It was taking too long to vent.

Good idea.

Press the shitter valve.

Wrong.

Blew shit all over me.

Left an impression of me on the bulkhead.

Went back on the casing.

Trot sentry couldn't stop laughing.

He thought I had measles.

The Bus ride

Gen

Me and my mate, John *'borrowed'* a USAF bus on Diego Garcia.

Well, what do you expect?

Fancy leaving a bus sitting there, doors open and keys in the ignition.
Someone could have stolen it FFS.

Anyway, we took it for a spin down the jetty... and I mean a spin... showing-off by doing some handbrake turns in front of the duty watch.

As fun as it was for a while, it is hard work manoeuvring a lumbering great bus, so we ditch it by the side of the road and clambered back on board to get our heads down.

The following day, the cox'n asked who took the bus.
We had to own up.

After all, half the ships company witnessed our antics the night before.
We were guessing this would be a hats and wellies job.

BUT, to our surprise and relief, the Yanks did not seem to mind us *'borrowing'* the bus.

Their only request was *'next time'*, would we please return the vehicle and park it in the same location where we found it.

One of the bessie days ever.

The Lemonade factory

Gen

The City of Liverpool

O n a T boat having a jolly, in sunny Liverpool.

The day before we were due to sail, we were invited to tour a lemonade factory, err, lemonade, yep that fizzy sweet stuff you love as a kid.

Of course, very few turned up for that exped.

I think there was only about eight or nine of us in the end.

However, it turned out the factory's governors had pulled out all the stops for us.

There was a shed load of beer and more strippers than guests.

A great time was had by all, especially a young WEM.

He came back dressed in one of the stripper's baby doll nightdress and nowt else. He went straight to his room and crashed out.

Problem was, the room he found was not his, nor one of anybodys on the boat.

His roommate thought he had gone back onboard but was that pissed forgotten to take his gear with him.

So, being helpful, his oppo brought it all back to the boat for him.

Now...

A short while after we sailed...

Our young WEM wakes up in the Feathers hotel in Liverpool, wearing a pink nightdress with a feather bower trim and nothing else.

Not even a pair of flipflops.

Apparently, the hotel staff were helpful and called the police.

They were also very helpful and gave our young WEM a blanket and a free ride back to Guzz.

The Navy. In its indomitable wisdom, then decided to also help him, by making his wallet £500 lighter.

Liverpool, great run if you ask me and a place that gave me a new-found love of lemonade... for a while.

The new Bloke

Joke

After my time in the Mob, I worked on a tramper plying trade from Scotland to Southern Spain.

The ship's company were a bunch of losers, chancers and neer-do-wells. Many keeping a low profile from the law.

But as a ship's company we were a tight-knit group, a group who did not take kindly to change or strangers.

So, when the Skipper took on a new bloke, the fellow was not best welcomed onboard.

The Skipper told the crew the bloke, "had seagoing experience and that he was an honest chap".

Give the new bloke his due, he was a grafter. He scrubbed and cleaned the decks continuously without complaint.
However, he was still not *'one of us'* and was still viewed with much suspicion.

It was about our third week at sea when, as the new bloke was busy, head down, mopping the decks, a huge gopher washed him over the side.

The first mate runs to the wheelhouse and calls to the Captain. "You know that new bloke, the one you said was honest?"

The Skipper nodded "Yes, what about him".

"Well," said the Mate, "His just fucked off and taken your mop with him!"

Swimming chickens

Gen-ish?

T.B. our Chief cook was given a shed load of frozen meat by a septic in Ashuabar, (a Kuwaiti port), at the end of the first Gulf War.

It was a load of frozen Rib Eye steaks, lamb chops and some boxes of chicken, which were beginning thaw.
Erring on the side of caution, we thought it best to ditch the Chuckies, not wanting to risk giving anyone salmonella.

Waiting until after we sailed and giving us enough time to be well clear of the port, we ditched the oven ready, half thawed, clukkers over the side, dutifully storing the cardboard boxes in the gash pile, where it would eventually, supposedly, go to some recycling plant.

However, unbeknown to us, being kept in the proverbial dark and fed great quantities of shite, like effing mushrooms, we were NOT sailing away from Kuwait City, but circling overnight... just offshore.

The following morning, about 09.00, T.B. the chief cook got a call to the upper deck, where the supply officer was standing with a bemused look on his face.

Glancing at T.B. the S.O. nodded towards the 'oggin.

Looking out to sea T.B. could see around 150 oven-ready chickens bobbing about on the ocean waves, all still cosily wrapped in their plastic Burberrys.

Without a moment's hesitation, T.B. simply shrugged and said, "It's steak night tonight, sir."

Tommo

On Tap Tommo, a legend, who was also known as *"Tommo the Amazing"*

Ovens came alongside 4 days early due to a defect, so a certain LSMT decided to have a few days on the piss instead of going home.

Unfortunately for this LSTM, whose wife was an ABMTD (*Driver*) at another establishment, two days after we got in said Wifey got a job which brought her down to Plats.

"Oh, how nice," she thought, hubby's boat is back; I'll pop down and see him, promise him all sorts of erotic delights when he gets home tonight.

Unfortunately...

While speaking with the Trot Sentry she was informed the boat had been back for two days.

Now, the young wife became a little annoyed and transformed into a screaming banshee, demanding to have her husband brought to the casing, so she can tear the rat into little pieces of shite.

This is where I come into the story...

I was returning from inboard when I spied wifey, steam pouring from her ears and raging red-faced, now standing on the casing.
I immediately realised the LSTM's few days of freedom have come to an abrupt end.

I calmed the wife down, well, I stopped her screaming quite as loud and I had the LSTM piped to the casing.

As you would expect, the unexpected and unscheduled presence of wifey spread like wildfire and, after several pipes with no LSTM showing his face, I set off to find him

After much searching I found the husband hiding in the Bear Pit. His begging and pleading were to no avail.

I ordered him to the casing to face his missus.

By this time an interested audience had gathered and waited with baited breath to see how the LSTM would fare against the challenge confronting him.

It was an amazing sight to behold.

A petit AB dragging a six-foot-four inch, hairy arsed, three badge leading seaman across the brow by his ear.

Neither is it often for an entire ships company of matelots to learn several new swear words in such a short space of time.

I do not think he was going to enjoy any form of bedroom gymnastics that night, of for many nights to come.

Tarring Jack

As a junior seaman on Tiger in 64/65 and an OD to boot, I'd heard you could still have a pigtail if you requested, so I did.

I was hauled in front of the OOD before being passed on, to the Commanders table, where I was informed my request was granted and the Chief GI would sort out the terms.

I left the table under instruction to be on the quarterdeck for tarring the following morning and every morning thereafter, at call the hands.

The Chief GI said, after the tarring session I would be escorted to another deck to pray to Mecca, (no idea why they dreamed that one up).

Anyway, to cut a long story short, I withdrew my request to grow a pigtail.

After my request was public knowledge, I, of course, endured weeks of being wound at every opportunity.

For example, it seemed I always needed my haircut, often twice a day.

Mind you the ship's barber became fed up of seeing me faster than I did seeing him.

He had a word in the appropriate shell-like and my frequent visits ceased.

Eventually, things returned to the relative state of normality and the ship's company found other things to focus their minds on.

The Newsagents trip

Joke

J ack popped out one Friday afternoon to get a paper and some tobacco from the local shop.

Now, you know how things are...one thing often leads to another and time sort of slips away.

Especially after a pint or two, when you bump into an old oppo and decide to have a beer together.

Jacks short walk to the newsagents turned into a weekend session. He did not return home until Monday night, after he spent all his money.

In fact, she was rather irritated.

After two hours of verbally berating Jack, she asked him how he would feel if he did not see her for three days.

Jack, being Jack, simply shrugged and said nonchalantly, "that would be fine with me."

All of Tuesday passed and Jack did not see his wife.
Neither did he see her on Wednesday or Thursday.

By Friday the swelling from his blackened eyes reduced enough for him to catch a glimpse of her from the corner of his left eye.

A Birthday Bang

Here is a rather modern take on the traditional dit. I'm told its Gen, but I'll let you decide.

You may recall when it all kicked off in Libya, when some chap called Colonel Gadhafi lost control of his country, his arse and his life? It was way back in 1986 when I was little more than a sprog.

At the time I was on HMS *****. It was my first seagoing draft. We were part of a small flotilla in the Med, patrolling the North African coast.

It was coming up to my birthday and I was looking forward to a mad piss-up with some of me old mates.

But that idea got fucked pretty quickly when the Libyan shitstorm started.

We were ordered to stay bobbing about in the Med, just off the Libyan coast, in case... in case of what no fucker told me.

Anywayhow, my mother knew (*way before we did*), I was not coming home for another few weeks or at least until all this uprising stuff settled down a bit.

It was part of something they now call the 'Arab Spring'. It was like all of a sudden, the whole Arab world was going bloody bonkers.

There were a ton of people trying to cross the Med in paddling pools and riding blow-up crocodiles they nicked from the bombed-out hotels. Others were forced to pay gunmen, to be crammed onto shitty boats that could hardly float and towed out to sea before being abandoned.

Half the people were running for their lives, scared shitless some fucker was going to blow their heads off; the other half were the fuckers who wanted to blow their heads off.

Both were all mixed together in a sweaty pile of crap floating in the middle of the bloody sea which made it impossible to tell who was who, who was running scared and who was ready to put a hole in your head or a knife in your back.

Most of them were hell-bent on getting to England, so they could blow our fucking country to smithereens until it looked like the shit hole dump they had just come from.

Like I said it was all a bit fucked up at that time.

The biggest trouble was no fucker knew which ones were bloody which, so the soft shite politicians we have let them all into country anyway.

WTF!

With all this crap going on all over, everybody was a bit edgy, so when the birthday card my mother sent me arrived at BFPO and the security scanner picked up the microchip inside, the stupid fuckers panicked, thinking it was a bomb, the chip being a trigger device, they blew the fucking thing up... a 'controlled explosion', as they called it.

Fact was, it was a musical card which simply played 'Happy Birthday' when opened.

So, thank you BF(fucking)PO, I never did get my birthday card that year, nor the effing twenty quid note me dad slipped inside it.

By the time I got home my birthday was long passed and no one gave a flying fuck that I missed the chance of a right good piss-up.

It rained every day during my leave, my girlfriend dumped me and ran off with the ugly fat lezzer from three doors down.

At the end of my leave, just as I was jumping on the train back to Pompey, my old man said he was skint, after backing another three-legged donkey no doubt, and could I lend him back the twenty quid he sent me for my birthday.

FFS.

Rant over.

As you were.

EPILOGUE

IT SEEMS A SHAME THIS BOOK MUST COME TO AN END BUT COME TO AN END IT MUST.

THE NUMBER OF DITS JACK HAS TOLD OVER THE YEARS ARE ALMOST ENDLESS. THERE ARE MANY MORE TALES THAN EVER THE NUMBER OF SAILORS.

WHICH, ON CONSIDERATION, IS NOT SURPRISING.
LIFE ABOARD SHIP PROVIDED AN ONGOING SOURCE FOR ORIGINATING STORIES.

WITH HUNDREDS OF MEN, TONS OF MILITARY PARAPHERNALIA, COMPLICATED MACHINERY, TECHNOLOGICAL EQUIPMENT, WEAPONRY, STORES AND VARIOUS OTHER FORMS OF KIT, YOU COULD BE ASSURED THAT NOT EVERY DAY WAS STRAIGHTFORWARD AND UNDEMANDING.

EQUIPMENT FAILED.

PEOPLE MADE MISTAKES.

ACCIDENTS AND MISHAPS OCCURRED.

PERSONALITIES AND CHARACTERS CLASHED.

ADD TO THIS MIX THE ACTIVITIES OF MATELOTS ON A 'RUN ASHORE' IN THOSE FAR-FLUNG, UNSAVOURY AND QUESTIONABLE SEAPORTS. INCLUDE BEER, SPIRITS, WINE, WOMEN AND SONG INTO THE EQUATION AND THE RESULTING CONCOCTION IS A WONDERFUL HOTHOUSE FOR THE CREATION OF IMAGINATIVE NARRATIVE.

THE GOINGS-ON, FROM BOTH ABOARD AND ASHORE, CREATED ASTONISHING ACCOUNTS OF EVENTS TO BE TOLD AT STAND EASY OR AFTER A WATCH; WHEN THE EXAGGERATED TELLING'S OF THE DAY'S HAPPENINGS WOULD BE SHARED IN THE MESS SQUARE.

THESE TALES WERE SHARED FROM MESS TO MESS, SHIP TO SHIP AND, AS IS THE NORM OF ALL VERBATIM DISCOURSES, THE STORIES BECAME ALTERED, ENHANCED AND ENRICHED EACH TIME THEY WERE CONVEYED, UNTIL THE ORIGINAL BASIS AND THE TRUE FACTS BECAME LOST IN THE MISTS OF MYTH AND FICTION.

THUS, THE CREATION OF A DIT.
CLEARLY, IT IS IMPOSSIBLE TO INCLUDE ALL THE DITS EVER SPUN IN A SINGLE BOOK. TO ATTEMPT TO DO SO WOULD CREATE A TOME LARGER AND HEAVIER THAN WAR AND PEACE... I PRESUME.

JACK'S DITS IS SIMPLY A SMALL SAMPLE, AN ILLUSTRATIVE REPRESENTATION OF THE PLETHORA OF DITS WHICH CIRCULATED WITHIN THE MESS DECKS OF ROYAL NAVY SHIPS.

MAYBE, JUST MAYBE, I SHALL CONTINUE TO COLLECT AND COLLATE THESE DITS. YOU NEVER KNOW, THERE COULD BE ANOTHER JACK'S DITS BOOK IN THE OFFING?

HAPPY DAYS.

PAUL [*KNOCKER*] WHITE.

AFTERWORD

THANK YOU FOR READING **JACKS DIT'S**
I TRUST THESE MESS DECK TALES STIMULATED YOUR OWN
MEMORIES OF THE 'GOOD TIMES'... I DO HOPE SO.

YOU MIGHT LIKE TO READ MY SHORT STORY COLLECTION, A SERIES
OF THREE BOOKS CALLED **TALES OF CRIME & VIOLENCE.**
AVAILABLE AS VOLUMES 1, 2 & 3, FROM AMAZON, CREATESPACE &
OTHER OUTLETS, AS PAPERBACKS OR ON KINDLE.

TALES OF CRIMES & VIOLENCE LOOKS DEEPER INTO THE HUMAN
PSYCHE, THE MIND AND SPIRITS OF THOSE INVOLVED.

ARE THEY THE PERPETRATORS OR THE VICTIMS? THE INNOCENT
CAUGHT IN THE CROSSFIRE, OR IS THERE MORE TO THEIR PRESENCE
THAN MEETS THE EYE? MAYBE THEY ARE WILLING PARTICIPANTS, OR
HAVE BEEN FORCED OR COERCED INTO TAKING PART?
FANCY SOMETHING A LITTLE LIGHT-HEARTED?

MY FULL-LENGTH NOVEL, **THE ABDUCTION OF RUPERT DEVILLE**
SHOULD BE RIGHT UP YOUR STREET.

RUPERT IS A LOST SOUL, A BUMBLING LAD, STAGGERING THROUGH
DAILY LIFE WHEN HE MEETS CARLA. IN THE MORNING OF THE DAY
HE IS TO PROPOSE, RUPERT IS SNATCHED OFF THE STREET... AND
HIS ADVENTURES BEGIN.

"THE ABDUCTION OF RUPERT DEVILLE IS A BOOK WHICH TRANSCENDS GENRE.

LIKE A GREAT PAINTING OR A WONDERFULLY COMPOSED PIECE OF MUSIC, PAUL HAS MANAGED TO MIX AND BLEND THE VARIOUS DISCIPLINES OF HIS ART INTO ONE AMAZING NOVEL.

IS 'THE ABDUCTION OF RUPERT DEVILLE' A SUSPENSE MYSTERY, YES. BUT IT IS ALSO A THRILLER, A ROMANCE OF LOVE, A HUMOROUS TOME, A STORY OF FINDING ONESELF AND MUCH MORE."

WHATEVER TYPE OF BOOK YOU REGULARLY READ, I SUGGEST YOUR NEXT BOOK BE THIS ONE.

"I HAD TO KEEP TURNING THE PAGES BECAUSE THIS BOOK MADE ME CRY. I HAD TEARS RUNNING DOWN MY CHEEKS, NOT ONLY FROM THE EMOTIONS WHICH PAUL CAN PORTRAY SO WELL BUT ALSO FROM THE LAUGHTER CAUSED BY THE MOST ABSURD SITUATIONS WHICH, ON OCCASION, THE CHARACTERS FIND THEMSELVES INVOLVED."

PLEASE, DO NOT HAVE ANY PRECONCEPTIONS ABOUT THE ABDUCTION OF RUPERT DEVILLE, JUST GET YOURSELF A COPY AND READ IT.

FIVE STARS ALL ROUND FROM ME."

ANDY PETERSON.

ABOUT THE AUTHOR

PAUL WHITE IS A PROLIFIC STORYTELLER, A WORDSMITH, TALE WEAVER AND AN AMAZON INTERNATIONAL BESTSELLING AUTHOR.

HE WRITES FROM HIS YORKSHIRE HOME, SITUATED NEAR A QUIET MARKET TOWN IN THE EAST RIDINGS.

PAUL HAS PUBLISHED SEVERAL BOOKS, FROM FULL-LENGTH NOVELS TO SHORT STORY COLLECTIONS, POETRY, CHILDREN'S BOOKS AND NON-FICTION, MILITARY SOCIAL HISTORY.

HE IS ALSO A CONTRIBUTOR TO VARIOUS COLLECTIVE ANTHOLOGIES.

YOU CAN FIND OUT MORE ABOUT PAUL, HIS WORKS-IN-PROGRESS, ARTWORKS AND OTHER PROJECTS, BY VISITING HIS WEBSITE:

HTTP://PAULZNEWPOSTBOX.WIX.COM/PAUL-WHITE

Books

FICTION

The Abduction of Rupert DeVille
(Paperback & Ebook)

Miriam's Hex
(Ebook only)

Tales of Crime & Violence
(Volumes 1, 2 & 3)

Dark Words – Dark Tales, Darker Poetry
(Paperback only)

Semi-Fiction

Life in the War Zone
(Paperback only)

Poetry

Teardrops & White Doves
(Paperback & Outsized Hardcover)

Shadows of Emotion
(Paperback & Ebook)

Military Social History

HMS Tiger -Chronicles of the last big cat
(Outsized Hardcover only)

The Pussers Cook Book
(Paperback & Hardcover)

Jack's Dits
(Paperback)

PAUL WHITE

CHILDREN'S STORIES

THE RABBIT JOKE
(OUTSIZED HARDCOVER)

A TREASURE CHEST OF CHILDREN'S STORIES
(ANTHOLOGY)

MUSIC / ART

ICONIC
(HARDCOVER)

ANTHOLOGIES
(JOINT AUTHOR / CONTRIBUTOR)

AWETHORS ANTHOLOGY – *LIGHT VOLUME*

AWETHORS DECEMBER ANTHOLOGY – *DARK VOLUME*

INDIVIDUALLY TOGETHER
(STORY BOOK PUBLISHING)

VIOLENCE, CONTROL & OTHER KINDS OF LOVE
(ABYSSINIAN PRESS)

LOOKING INTO THE ABYSS
(TOAD PUBLISHING)

A TREASURE CHEST OF CHILDREN'S STORIES
(PLAISTED PUBLISHING HOUSE)

MIDSUMMER ANTHOLOGY

(JARA PUBLISHING)

ONE LAST THING

I WOULD LIKE TO LEAVE YOU WITH THIS, THE AUTHOR I AM SORRY TO SAY, IS UNKNOWN.

THE DEMISE OF JACK TAR

The traditional male sailor was not defined by his looks. He was defined by his attitude.

His name was Jack Tar. He was a happy go lucky sort of bloke. He took the good times with the bad.

He didn't cry victimisation, bastardisation, discrimination or for his mum when things didn't go his way.

He took responsibility for his own sometimes, self-destructive actions.

He loved a laugh at anything or anybody. Rank, gender, race, creed or behaviour, it didn't matter to Jack.

He would take the piss out of anyone, including himself. If someone took it out of him he didn't get offended. It was a natural part of life. If he offended someone else, so be it.

Free from many of the rules of a polite society Jack's manners were somewhat rough.

His ability to swear was legendary

Jack loved women. He loved to chase them to the ends of the earth and sometimes he even caught one (less often than he would have you believe though). His tales of the chase and its conclusion win or lose, is the stuff of legends.

Jack's favourite drink was beer, and he could drink it like a fish. His actions when inebriated would, on occasion, land him in trouble. But, he took it on the chin, did his punishment and then went and did it all again.

Jack loved his job. He took an immense pride in what he did. His radar was always the best in the fleet. His engines always worked better than anyone else's. His eyes could spot a contact before anyone else's and shoot at it first.

It was a matter of personal pride. Jack was the consummate professional when he was at work and sober. He was a bit like a mischievous child. He had a gleam in his eye and a larger than life outlook.

He was as rough as guts. You had to be pig headed and thick skinned to survive. He worked hard and played hard. His masters tut-tutted at some of his more exuberant expressions of joie de vivre, and the occasional bout of number 9's or stoppage of leave let him know where his limits were.

The late 20th Century and on, has seen the demise of Jack. The workplace no longer echoes with ribald comment and bawdy tales. Someone is sure to take offence.

Whereas, those stories of daring do and ingenuity in the face of adversity, usually whilst pissed, lack the audacity of the past. A wicked sense of humour is now a liability, rather than a necessity. Jack has been socially engineered out of existence.

What was once normal is now offensive. Denting someone else's over inflated opinion of their own self-worth is now a crime.

END

Printed in Great Britain
by Amazon